Morning Mocha Press

Yakima, Washington

ISBN:978-1-7338244-6-0

Cover Design: Carpe Librum Book Design

The Rancher's Resilient Heart

APPLE VALLEY RANCHERS
BOOK TWO

DALYN WELLER

The Rancher's Resilient Heart

For Teresa.

You showed me what true resilience looks like.

"The Lord is the one who will go before you. He will be with you; he will not leave you or abandon you. Do not be afraid or discouraged."

Deuteronomy 31:8 CSB

Contents

Chapter 1

DUMPED AND BITTEN

Evan McClure shuffled the invoices and contracts stacked eyeball high on his desk. He shouldn't have let the ranch business get so behind, but he hated office work. He'd have to get used to it sooner or later since it was all he was fit for now.

He rubbed the swollen, raw stump where his leg used to be. He couldn't even use his crutches, sore as he was from yet another ill-fitting prosthetic. With a temperament like an aggravated hornet, he'd shut himself inside today to avoid being belligerent to the cowboys who were doing the real work.

He swiveled to investigate a scuffling noise in the doorway.

"Uncle Evan, one of the cattle dogs had pups in the small barn. Wanna go see 'em with us?" Bella's eyes danced and

Theo, standing beside her, bounced on the balls of his feet with a grin locked on his face.

"Wish I could, but I'm busy sortin' out money."

Bella crossed her arms and scowled. "Lindy Harper says our family is richer than God, so why are you bothering with all that?" Her gaze swept Evan's desk.

She was sassy, that one. "Well," he began in a slow drawl, "if we don't keep accounts, pretty soon the money will dry up, and we won't be able to afford your fancy ponies." He rounded his eyes and feigned a look of concern.

Theo's eyes widened, but Bella just lifted one brow in a perfect imitation of her mother and stalked off, calling for Theo to follow her.

Chuckling, Evan turned his chair toward the window. Maybe it was time for a break.

Outside, he wheeled down the ramp and headed for the barn to meet Bella and Theo. He should have just agreed to go see the puppies with them in the first place.

A flash of sorrel hide caught his eye. The fancy new stud they'd bought from an outfit in Texas must have arrived. A new horse was far more interesting than a puddle of pups. He wheeled himself to the round pen on the other side of the barn. It was slow going, trying to avoid stones and mud. Once he got to the wooden rails, he pulled himself up to admire Grandpa Smokey's newest equine acquisition.

The stallion was magnificent. His coat gleamed like it was made of liquid. Evan cocked an ear. The ranch was quiet with everyone gone to sort cattle, but the horse was tacked up. In one of his saddles. That gave him a pang in his gut. He hadn't ridden in years, and it was all he'd ever wanted to do since he was old enough to toddle to a hitching post.

He dropped into his chair and wheeled back a few feet, craning his neck in every direction. Even the interns were gone. An idea stoppered his wind, made his heart sound like hoofbeats in his ears. If this was his life, he might as well start living it, because he wasn't going to sprout a new leg.

He hopped to the gate and unlatched it, catching the sorrel's reins. He stroked the horse's neck, held his head to meet soft, brown eyes, and then ran a hand down his hindquarters. The stallion flared his nostrils and snorted but stood without flinching.

Evan checked the cinch, tightened it, and hoisted himself up before he could second guess his decision. He'd forgotten the view from horseback. The sun kissed his face, and he tipped back to soak it up. But before he had the chance to open his eyes, his neck whipped back with a crack and the wind was kissing his face instead. The horse had bolted through the gate Evan had left open, and they were headed for the dirt road.

An exhilarating rush of blood pumped through Evan as if it came straight from the horse's heart to his own. He'd missed a good gallop. He tried to rein the horse left so they could ride to the hills, but the stallion fought the bit. Evan, unbalanced as he was, slid sideways. The horse pinned his ears, tucked his head between his front feet, and bucked. Evan clung to the saddle horn while the horse kicked, reared, and bucked like fury. And then Evan was air born, tossed sideways against a tree. With a bone-jarring crunch, he hit the trunk and slid down.

Stunned, he lay still trying to take stock of what was left of his body. With a groan, he lifted his face out of the dirt and spat out a clump of who-knew-what. A trickle of something wet and warm blurred his vision.

Blood.

He wiped it away with a shaky hand but froze at something shaking behind him. Oh-so-slowly, he turned his head. His entrails tangled at the sight of the gray coils.

A rattler.

"Lord, I know I've been mighty ungrateful about this business of livin' without my leg, but if—"

"Hey! What in the—" Dad stomped toward him.

Evan threw up a hand to ward him off. "Son-of-a-biscuit-eater!" The snake struck at his sudden move. "Call Seth Hanson. I need a chopper out." His voice was raspy. He hadn't quite got his wind back from being tossed.

Dad snatched up a long stick and beat the ground until the snake slithered off. "You bit, son?" He tossed the stick and knelt at Evan's side, his brows pinched together.

Nodding, Evan grimaced. "Hurts worse than a kick to the head. Make that call, would you? I could die here in the dirt while you're asking questions."

Call made, Dad squared off with him. "What were you doin' on that horse? And without your prosthetic?"

"Could we talk later? Like, at the hospital? I'm feelin' a little sick here."

"You bet we're gonna talk. While we're in Seattle, you're going to have a chat with that surgeon finally, too. Osseointegration is the only option if you're determined to be a cowboy again."

Dizzy and nauseated, Evan had to concede. But if the implant didn't take—if the bone wouldn't grow around it, that would leave him with no options. And that would leave him without hope.

LIBBY HALVERSON PULLED her Jeep into a vacant spot on the side of the horse barn near the Three M ranch house. She cut the engine and watched as a frisky pair of calves acted up in a turnout with half a dozen well-bred colts. The McClures raised their ranch geldings with cattle. Smart. One of many reasons their breeding program was successful.

They had more than just the horses. Fruit orchards, hay, and beef added to the ranch's overall success. The McClures were called "gold fingers" in their small community of Apple Valley. It was one of the reasons she'd kept her distance from the Three M after her father left them high and dry. Being poor was embarrassing.

So was unrequited love.

Libby gulped a steadying breath before she got out of her Jeep. "Stay here, Pumpkin. I'm not sure if you're welcome inside." She patted the geriatric Golden Retriever and slipped her a treat. April weather was unpredictable in the high desert, but even so, she rolled the windows down halfway. Pumpkin became anxious when she couldn't stick her long, orange nose out.

Molly, Libby's younger sister, had married into the McClure clan. She lived here, but Libby avoided visiting most of the time. She preferred to meet Molly at their family farmhouse or their mother's bookstore in town. The Books & Brew was the best place to get coffee and it was the only bookstore for fifty miles. Besides, she loved it. The smell of coffee and books together were nearly as nice as horse sweat and leather.

Evan McClure, her private pay patient—and former crush —was waiting in that log mansion, two weeks out from surgery, and itching to start rehab, according to his wealthy, cash-paying father.

Was she ready for Evan McClure?

She sat straighter. Maybe she should be asking if Evan was ready for her.

Truth was, it hurt to see him in a wheelchair.

He'd been the most handsome, most popular boy in their high school once upon a time. Evan had excelled in every sport, was nice to the nerds, and probably rescued stray puppies. He might as well have worn a superhero cape. But when he'd enlisted in the Army after high school, Libby had been relieved. Her heart had taken a fresh hit every time she'd seen him with Angela Macy. Angela had been the prettiest girl in school as well as the loosest if rumors were to be believed. Libby had chosen to believe them.

Years had gone by before she'd seen Evan again. In a

wheelchair. Minus a leg. The former town Superman—a combat-wounded veteran. Her heart had clambered right up her throat at her first sight of him. Guilt over wishing Evan gone had edged out her compassion.

She was ashamed of that.

When Grandma Rose asked her to do a favor for her old friend, Smokey McClure, she'd never dreamed it had anything to do with Evan. But she contracted to work his rehabilitation after Osseointegration surgery because she was lonely traveling around for work and she wanted a reason to come home. Besides, the job gave her a chance to work off some of her guilt where Evan was concerned. There was little chance he ever gave her a second thought, but she'd never quite gotten over that cowboy.

And veterans were her specialty. It would give her professional satisfaction to see him in his former glory, a man who could outwork, outplay, and out-shine everybody else.

The memory of Evan slumped in a wheelchair, thin and diminished in every way, made her squirm. If she could help— even a little bit—to restore him to the man he used to be, it would go a long way in helping her recover, too. After losing a combat-wounded veteran she'd been working with all winter to suicide, she'd nearly quit her vocation.

"Libby?" A deep, familiar voice called her name from the porch.

Her heart skipped a beat. Super annoying. She couldn't do her job if she was going to react like a teenager every time she was near Evan. She tried to tell her heart that high school was in the past and carrying over a crush on the star quarterback was ridiculous.

She was going to remain professional.

She shielded her eyes against the late afternoon sun. *Keep your distance, Lib. That's the only way this is going to work.* "I'll be right there," she called to Evan. Then she sent up a long, silent prayer for strength.

She reached back in the passenger seat for her tote bag. "You be a good girl and take a nap, Pumpkin."

Pumpkin raised sad eyes and collapsed with a dramatic sigh on the back seat.

Inside the enormous house, Libby marveled at the polished log walls and log beamed ceilings. She followed Evan as he wheeled to a spacious room with a window overlooking a lake. Another window overlooked a swimming pool. She fingered a brindle cowhide casually thrown over an oversized chair, examined mounted elk and deer heads, touched the supple, dark leather chairs and sofas. Everything similar in style to furnishings in the western fashion magazines her sister, Josie, brought home. Of course, Josie was usually in those photos.

"Care for tea or lemonade?" Evan asked. "Mrs. Mulligan, our house manager, keeps us stocked."

Libby shook her head. "I won't stay long. I only came to check in and discuss a schedule for therapy and your independent exercises."

Evan nodded but she glimpsed a hint of disappointment in his eyes. Was he lonely cooped up on the ranch, recovering from yet another surgery? His tousled, dark brown hair was long enough to have little curls at the ends.

Libby licked dry lips. She was a trained professional. Not a friend. And certainly not the girl who had snagged Evan's forgotten sweatshirt from the football field in tenth grade.

She sat in a leather chair and unpacked her tote while he transferred himself from his wheelchair to the seat next to her. Once seated he peered at her with tired eyes and adjusted his bandaged stump on the matching ottoman.

He didn't look bad for a man who'd just endured his—she checked her notes—ninth surgery.

Libby pulled a short questionnaire out of the pile of paperwork she'd brought with her.

"Now then, let's talk about your goals and..." She blinked. A big screen TV flashed on the wall. "Is that..."

"*Curious George.* Don't judge. It's Theo's favorite. We were watching it together earlier." Evan pulled a remote control from underneath his rear and set it down on the side table.

She fended off a smile. Hard to imagine this larger-than-life former soldier slash cowboy watching a cartoon about a monkey and a guy wearing a yellow hat.

"Don't tell me you don't watch *Curious George?*" Evan said with mock horror. "We have to remedy that."

She laughed despite herself and fiddled around in her tote bag until she found her pen.

"I don't remember my—I mean our niece..." she stumbled over her words. It was awkward bringing up the past. "I don't remember Bella watching *Curious George* when she came to visit. She was more of a *My Little Pony* fan."

Evan's heart-melting grin reminded her of him as a shiny seventeen-year-old in his letterman's jacket with boots and spurs, not the smile of a man who'd nearly died in a foreign land where nobody knew how wonderful he was.

Retrieving a manilla folder, Libby fanned her warm face. "So, the surgery went well. Osseointegration is a marvel. We're going to work on flexibility, balance, and sharpening your coordination right away." She glanced up with a frown. "My notes say you were bitten by a snake a few months ago?"

"Weekend warrin'." Evan shrugged and slid a cushion under his bandaged stump. "I want you to know upfront that I'm okay with your tough approach."

Libby frowned. "Who said I was tough?"

"I've come to know a few wounded vets over the years."

"What do people say about me?" She leveled a glare his way.

"The truth?"

"Out with it. I can take it."

"Word is you drive your patients hard, but the results are worth it. They also say you're real easy on the eyes so it's hard to stay mad at you." Evan scrubbed a hand across the shadow of stubble on his jaw. "I can see where that might be a problem."

The twinkle in Evan's eyes threw her heart into high gear.

"Aunt Libby!" Bella's squeal interrupted the conversation. Thank goodness.

Libby turned to Bella just in time to catch her flying body as she hurtled herself in for a hug.

"I've missed you," Bella said.

"I've missed you too, kiddo. Where's your brother?"

"Theo's working with Grandma Rose in her garden today. Didn't you see him?"

"I must have just missed him. Why didn't you go to the farmhouse, too?"

"I wanted to stay and help Mom." She jerked her thumb behind her.

Molly shuffled in the great room in crumpled pajamas, her icy blond hair in a snarl. Purple shadowed the skin under her eyes. She gave Libby a wan smile and hoisted the youngest McClure onto her drooping shoulder.

Libby jumped up with her arms outstretched. "Oh, honey. You're exhausted. Let me take the baby."

"No. You're here to work with Evan. And yes, I am exhausted, but Cody is on his way back in from branding camp so I can have a nap. Rose was awake most of the night. She's teething."

Cody called a *halloo* from the doorway. Molly sagged in obvious relief. She may be tired, but she was happy.

Libby wouldn't mind being *that* tired if she could also be *that* happy.

Her job as a traveling physical therapist had kept her preoccupied. She'd met some wonderful men, but she would never put romance above her career. She never wanted to be as vulnerable as Mom had been after she'd been left with three daughters and debt piled to the rafters. Being the eldest, Libby remembered more than her sisters. Like the sound of Mom crying in her bedroom at night.

Besides, no one had ever inspired her to take the risk.

"Let me have my little rosebud." Evan reached for the red-faced baby, and Molly settled Rose in his lap. "Head upstairs and take a shower, sis. I'll keep Rosie with me until Cody washes up." Evan's eyes were soft and hungry.

Did he want what Cody had for himself someday?

"I can take her now," Cody offered. He snatched his hands back and gave Molly a sheepish look when she pointed to his filth-covered gloves. "Right. Shower first. Then you go to bed for a spell, Mama"

Something pinched Libby's heart at the way these men took care of her sister. She'd vowed to never rely on a man, but seeing Molly so loved, she wondered if keeping a fence around her heart was worth all the effort she'd given it.

Chapter 2

A WAGER

E van handed sleepy-eyed baby Rose to his brother after Cody came downstairs, hair still wet. Cody held the sleepy bundle of baby to his chest like a treasure and ushered his wife upstairs to rest with his hand on the small of her back.

Evan never knew how much he liked children—especially babies—until he'd become an uncle. He'd never admit it, but occasionally he'd catch himself gazing into Rose's face and imagine holding his own baby. He'd like to look into the face of an infant stamped with his features.

But that sort of happiness wasn't likely to be his. He'd had all his blessings when he was younger. His good fortune had bled out in the sand of a dusty little village in Afghanistan. That was the day he'd marked as the day God stopped smiling on him.

As he settled back in his chair it was hard not to notice that the sunlight streaming through the window made Libby's red-gold hair shimmer. The effect was distracting. So were her pale blue eyes. The gray rings around her irises were unusual. He'd always liked to look at them but never dared stare for fear of her catching him at it.

Evan fixed a benign smile on his face as Libby returned to her seat. She was brisk and business-like, but his senses tingled at her every move. The scent of lemons and soap hung in the air around her long, curly hair.

It was driving him nuts.

He was supposed to focus on making his goals. Working with her was going to be difficult, but not for the reasons he'd initially thought.

"You're not listening to me, Evan." Libby's exasperated tone pulled him back into the moment.

Libby used to be all legs and tangled mane. A bossy play-mate as a child. Seems the bossy part hadn't changed.

"I understand you tolerate bearing weight well, and your mobility has increased quite a bit since they placed the implant?"

"Yep. The surgeon says soon I'll be able to tell the differ-ence between walking on dirt or cement. The bone integration is a win for that reason alone."

"That would be a best-case scenario." Libby's smile reached her eyes, making them crinkle in the corners. "This is a list you should be familiar with." She handed him several pages with illustrated instructions of strength-building exer-cises. "These last two are modified to make allowance for the implant. I'll come for two hours a day to start, five days a week. That sets a grueling pace at first, but I'm confident it will mean the kind of progress you said you wanted." She held up the goal sheet he'd filled out with his surgeon several weeks ago. "We'll evaluate your progress at the end of two weeks and see how you feel then."

"I do all these already. I want to be back in the saddle as soon as possible."

"One day at a time, cowboy."

Evan lifted his chin. So what if he was stubborn? He was fighting to get his life back.

"You remember we have a cattle drive at the end of every summer? I want to be on it. By next year I'll be taking the lead. And one more thing, I invited my chapter of the Wounded Patriots to come to the ranch for a week in July. The ranch is a good place to get a break from life for the guys living in tighter spaces."

"Nice." She was using her serious therapist expression on him. "Those are lofty goals this early in the game, but it gives us something to shoot for. I believe goals are a vital part of recovery."

"Good. We agree then. I'd also like to compete in a roping event this fall."

"I don't think—"

"I'm not dumb enough to try to jump out of the saddle and chase a calf. But I am good with my hands." He paused for effect, but Libby didn't take the bait. He shrugged. His charm was rusty, that was all. "I'll be the header for team roping. I took up practice roping again last summer."

Libby pushed herself out of her chair and retrieved her bag. Her hair fell in a curtain of fiery gold. What would happen if he reached out to see if it was hot? He pressed his hands into the arms of the chair. Best not to risk another limb. Libby had two sides. The color of her hair was fair warning.

Libby cocked her head at him. "Still ambitious, I see."

He picked up his prosthetic leg along with the tool he used to screw it onto the implanted abutment. It had been two weeks since the surgery and as the bone grew around the implant, he'd experienced bone-gnawing aches. Like today.

He stood and stifled a groan. Beads of sweat trickled from his scalp. He'd known lots of guys who got hooked on pain pills. He wasn't going to be one of them.

Libby put a hand on his forearm. She applied pressure until he sat. "You're in pain." It was an accusation—not a question. "Are you staying on the schedule your surgeon prescribed for pain control?" Her hands were placed on either side of him, arms rigid, face so close he could smell the gum she was chewing.

He'd have to upset her more often.

"I don't have pain all the time. It's just that I've been pushing hard. I have the smallest hint of sensation on that side again—and trust me—I welcome it." He set his jaw. Her misplaced pity would prevent him from attacking his goals. He'd wasted too many years wallowing in it.

"Evan, the protocol is tailored to help you heal without becoming addicted to the pain meds." There was a glint in her eye. So she knew what worried him. But still… There was a glint in her eye.

Evan glared at her. "I've had more surgeries at this point than you've had birthdays."

She rolled her eyes. "Don't exaggerate."

He wanted to be angry, but those jeans fit her like a—

"Are you going to be reasonable?" She demanded.

"Probably not."

"You should try to reduce the inflammation at the implant site for a day or two before we work hard." She backed up and fished around in her bag again.

He should not be eyeballing the flattering cut of his therapist's jeans. Even if it was Libby Halverson.

"You have a whole team on your side. You aren't doing this alone." She faced him and jotted notes into the little notebook she carried. When she looked up, her eyes softened and she placed a hand on his right knee. "We will get you where you want to go."

"Thanks." Maybe if she took a few steps back and her hair didn't smell so nice he could think straight.

Maybe if she saw him as more of a man and less as a patient, he wouldn't feel so challenged.

Libby stepped away. "I'll be back tomorrow. We start at nine sharp." She pointed her finger. "But we won't go hard. We'll work on balance because that'll help you on the ground as well as in the saddle—later."

"Shoot…by the end of the summer, I'll be dancin' the Two-Step. I guarantee you that." He winked at Libby.

She tilted her head with a challenge in her eye. "Care to bet on that brag, cowboy?"

The perfect opening. Evan leaned back in the chair, folded his hands on his abs, and grinned a wolf smile. "I do. You said you encourage goals for recovery?"

"I did." Her eyes narrowed.

"Well then. Suppose if I can dance the Two-Step by August, you agree to attend the Cattlemen's Ball with me in a pretty blue dress. One that matches your eyes."

"That's not really the kind of bet I meant. The stakes are a bit—"

"High? Or do you mean it's not professional? Maybe you'd rather not dance with a one-legged cowboy?"

"You don't believe that." Flustered, she crossed her arms over her chest and scowled. Even her scowl was pretty. "You should know that the reason I work with veterans—specifically combat-wounded amputees—is because I'm proud of your sacrifice and bravery."

Libby lifted her chin. "Seems you're still fond of a wager. I accept your bet. But if you aren't dancing by August, you have to donate a big fat chunk of money to the equine therapy program I plan to start."

He had no idea what she was talking about, but something inside his belly did a little jig at accepting a bet with such a nice reward attached. "I'd gladly donate to that cause. Won't even have to lose a bet to write the check."

The left side of her mouth quirked upward but she didn't actually smile.

"I accept your terms. Dancing by August...say the eleventh?"

Libby shrugged. "Three months? Okay. But why that date?"

"That's my Alive Day."

"Your alive—oh." Her brows pulled into a frown. "The day of the explosion?"

"It was a good day, only I didn't recognize it for a year or three. PTSD is... well, it's much worse than an Osteointegration surgery." He gave her a crooked grin.

"I'm glad you came home, Evan. I really am." She turned pink, snagged her bag, and fled the room before he could reply.

Libby sure did blush a lot. Evan grinned with a renewed surge of determination. He had another goal to add to his private list.

"I'll be dancing by the end of summer, and you'll look like a dream on my arm."

"Who are you talking to?" Seth Hanson asked. His best friend since high school, they'd enlisted and served together in the same platoon. Seth had come home intact—mostly.

Evan rose and tugged his pant leg down over his prosthetic. "Who let you in?"

Seth wore a sly grin. "Libby Halverson came out just as I reached the door. I can't believe your dad hired her. What's he punishing you for this time?" He strolled across the room, his eyes—as always—sharp and measuring.

More than anyone aside from Dad, Seth had kept vigil

over Evan after he'd come home and burrowed into a depression so deep no one could reach him. Not even God. Evan had resented Seth's presence then. The intrusion had prevented him from going completely dark. Thank God for Seth.

It was dangerous being alone in the darkest part of your soul.

"Seriously, Libby may be easy on the eyes, but she's gonna be hard on your ego." Seth reached out a lightning-quick hand to steady Evan as he wobbled.

"I'm not worried." Evan shook Seth's grip off his forearm. "What could be harder than getting blown-up?"

"Your confidence does you credit. However, it's misplaced." Seth's eyes mocked him the way they always did when they gave each other a hard time.

Evan had no intentions of allowing Libby—or any other woman—to put his heart through a meat grinder again. But he couldn't deny something of his old self was stirring.

He welcomed it.

Was he worried about Libby's light blue eyes, flecked with gray, robbing him of a little pride?

Maybe a bit, but not enough to stop flirting with her.

LIBBY PACED in the shadows of the barn. What had she been thinking? Making a wager with a patient was one thing. But betting him for a date? She could not attend the Cattlemen's

Ball with Evan McClure. And not because he had a prosthetic leg. He didn't really believe that, did he?

The ball was a long way off. She'd think of something by August. She had every intention of seeing Evan dancing.

Just not with her.

Mom's flock of Sebastopol geese honked, making an ear-splitting racket when Pumpkin trotted through their ranks.

"Here you are." Mom was breathless but smiling. "Grandma Rose said you were in the barn putting the halter on Dolly Llama." Mom scooted the geese out of her way, pulled her hair back, tied it in a knot, and unwound the hose from its reel. "I came to fill their pool. You'd think they'd be more grateful."

Libby frowned at the gander who gave her poor dog a passing bite on the rear. "I'll turn it on when you're ready."

Pumpkin sniffed the bum of the gander and got another bite on the nose when the bird turned around, clearly offended. The old retriever cried out and cowered behind Libby's legs.

"I guess what's good for the goose is not what's good for the gander." She soothed Pumpkin with a pat on her head. "Silly girl, don't mess with the geese."

"Poor thing." Mom's sympathetic tone brought Pumpkin's ears up. She slunk nearer for a scratch from Mom. "You're a sweet girl, aren't you?" Mom bent to let the dog burrow her head under her arm. "She's such a good companion to everyone. I'm glad you happened along in her life when you did. To think the owners were going to put her down." Mom's tone became indignant.

"I suppose the thought of an aging dog is off-putting to people raising young children. Pumpkin's previous owners were nice enough, they just seemed over-committed with their children's activities and their own careers."

"Hmmmph." Mom stood. "People who get cute puppies ought to know it's a lifelong commitment."

Mom loved animals, and her crowded farm was proof.

"I turned the spigot. You should have water now."

"Thanks, sweetie. Were you able to get the halter on Dolly Llama?"

"I got the halter on, but she wasn't happy about it. Didn't Gram say she brought that beast home for Bella and Theo?"

"That's what she claimed."

"But Dolly isn't a bit friendly."

"My mother is sure she will become a gentle and sweet unicorn with time. She's going to dress her in feather boas and pearls and make her wear hats."

Libby snorted. "No, but really."

"Really. The llama is her new hobby. Animal therapy. She's going to train pets and take them to nursing homes and hospitals."

"It sounds like animal cruelty. Has anyone told her she's unlikely to get Dolly Llama in an elevator? I mean, they aren't going to allow her to bring livestock inside the Apple Valley hospital."

A smile brushed Mom's lips. "You know my mother... she's always up to something." She arched a brow. "And she treats her pets very well." She patted Pumpkin and looked thoughtful. "Pumpkin might be a worthy candidate for pet therapy."

Libby stroked Pumpkin's head. "I'm worried Grandma Rose will be disappointed with her newest project. Dolly is not well-behaved. She's not even civil. She tried to spit on me."

"Grandma Rose is nothing if not resilient. Remember two years ago when she volunteered at the elementary school?"

"But quit because she didn't like their lunches." Libby tightened the lid on a grain bin. "And I remember when she was going to be a travel writer and start a blog."

"Only she doesn't like to travel." Mom laughed.

"And she didn't own a computer. That was as short-lived as her yoga studio."

"I think Dolly Llama will tame down eventually. Especially if you get her halter trained so Theo and Bella can handle her." Mom filled the blue plastic pool and tossed the hose aside. "Turn off the water, please."

Libby turned the knob and rolled the hose onto its wheel. It was good to be back on the farm after so many hotel rooms and tiny apartments.

Stepping out of the way of the splashing geese, Mom touched Libby's arm. "How is Evan?"

"Why do you ask?" Libby's voice squeaked.

Mom squinted at her. "Umm…because I'm curious? The man had major surgery, after all."

Libby's face heated. "He's doing…he's fine."

"Good. I'm glad to hear it." She squatted to pet one of her geese.

The bird's feathers resembled Cinderella's ballgown, which brought the Cattlemen's Ball to mind. Should she tell Mom about her bet with Evan?

"Libby, is your heart going to be safe working with Evan?"

"That's a funny question. I'm his physical therapist."

"There was the sad incident with that poor Luke."

Why did her mom have to bring that up? Every medical professional lost a patient sometimes. Libby knelt to pick up a long, curly white goose feather.

"You had a crush on Evan all through high school. Not that anyone could blame you. Every woman in Apple Valley with a daughter around your age complained about their girls fawning over him. Joyce Pence told everyone at a PTA meeting that her girls and their friends wrote his name all over their notebooks." She laughed. "I was complaining right along with the other moms."

"You knew?"

"I'm your mother. Of course, I knew." She tucked an errant strand of her blond hair behind her ear. The silver hoops dangling from her lobes glinted in the sun. They were a gift from Molly, their family's lady silversmith. They all wore pieces of her jewelry.

"I used to worry you'd cry yourself sick when Evan took up with Angela what's-her-name." Mom pulled a weed and tossed it in the rocks. "It was shameful the way she jilted him after he returned from Afghanistan."

Libby shrugged. "I suppose Angela figured she couldn't

handle what lay in store. Veterans who come home wounded can take a long time to heal. Inside and out. Some never do."

Libby's heart constricted. Luke Conner had never healed, and he'd ended up taking his own life.

"Are you talking about his missing leg or PTSD? Because he came home a different young man. The confident, capable man who left our valley never returned."

"Coming home with PTSD might just be tougher than losing a limb. Either way, I think soldiers leave part of themselves behind." Libby wiped mud from her hand, leaving streaks on her pant leg. "But Evan is capable of getting his shine back."

"Oh?" Mom's shrewd look reminded her to avoid breaking confidences with her patient.

"He's doing well with his implant. He's already walking in athletic shoes. He wants to try boots next."

"Leave it to Evan McClure to overachieve." Mom winked. "He's still a handsome man, and I'm still worried about you."

"Oh, please. I'm not a girl with a crush on the cutest boy in school anymore."

"You've never once had a serious boyfriend that I know about." Mom shot her a scrutinizing look.

"There was that one guy…" Libby tried to remember his name. He was an architect. Ate with his mouth open.

"Dating a man longer than a week doesn't count as serious in anyone's reckoning."

Libby put a flake of hay in the llama's feeder and shut the stall door. "Evan is my patient. *Only* my patient."

"Tell yourself comforting lies if you have to, but I'll bet you still have a tingle for him," Mom said. "It's not the worst thing you know."

"Please stop."

"Evan McClure is an eligible bachelor, a wealthy rancher, and he's great with kids. I'm team Evan all the way."

"Just a second ago you were saying he didn't come home right. Make up your mind." Libby glared. She brushed past Mom and headed for their farmhouse. "Come on, Pumpkin."

"People do heal," Mom called after her.

Mom had always had a soft spot for Evan. Especially since she'd had a flat tire in the snow on her way to work one winter morning. Evan had been home on leave, and he'd stopped to help her.

Libby went inside the house to find a snack.

Grandma Rose was in the kitchen playing the oldies on a little portable speaker. Her hips bounced back and forth to Elvis.

"It smells wonderful in here." Libby sniffed. "What are you baking?" She'd been too nervous to eat earlier. Now that her first appointment with Evan was over, she was ravenous.

"Cookies. The kids are coming tomorrow to help in my garden." Gram faced her. "Did you get that halter on Dolly Llama?"

"I did. I'm not sure she's ready for the kids yet, though. Or rather, that they are ready for her. She's spicy."

"Good. She'll fit right in around here." Gram wiped her

hands and flicked the tip of her wet dishtowel in the direction of Libby's rear.

"Hey!" Libby protested. She snatched a cookie from the cooling rack.

Gram shot her a glare but slid another cookie toward her. The turquoise rings on her fingers clacked on the rack.

Libby pointed to Gram's hand. "How do work with all those on?"

"Fast." She slipped a loaded cookie pan into the oven. Straightening with a groan, she turned to Libby. "Was your mother interrogating you about working with young Evan?"

Libby sighed. "Not you, too."

Her phone chimed from her back pocket. "Thanks for the snack," she called to Gram. Slipping her phone out, she headed upstairs to take the call. Pumpkin settled on the kitchen floor near Grandma Rose and the cookies cooling on the counter.

Chapter 3
WOUNDED PATRIOTS

Swimming worked the knots out of Evan's back and shoulders. The surgeon had cleared him for the pool if he wore a rubber sleeve on the implant site, so he'd taken to swimming every morning. He'd finished his laps and was toweling off when Libby's voice floated over the fence along with a cloud of dust from her Jeep. "Out of the way, dogs!"

Evan ran his fingers through damp, too-long hair and headed inside. He was overdue with his barber. Maybe Mrs. M would be willing to cut it again. He took the elevator upstairs to dress. After pulling on a T-shirt and some gym shorts, he stopped to smooth his unruly curls back and took a good, long look in his bathroom mirror. From the waist up nobody would know he'd been blown to bits.

Evan flicked off the lights and went down to meet Libby for P.T.

"There you are. Ready?" Libby set down a duffel. She

wore black yoga pants and a Three M T-shirt. She met his eyes and then looked down at the shirt. "Molly gave it to me."

The shirt looked good on her. "What's in there?" Evan pointed at the bag.

"Exercise bands. We're going to work your hips today."

An eyebrow waggle and a grin got him nothing. Libby was immune. "How about a coffee first? I haven't had any yet."

"No thanks, I've been up for hours. I got the bug to take my old jogging route. I can't believe I used to do that every day." Libby's flushed skin and sparkling eyes made it difficult for Evan to look anywhere else.

Her sparkle dimmed. "Let's get started." The bossy tone was back. Libby pulled her hair—curly and tangled—into a knot on top of her head, leaving her high cheekbones and throat exposed.

Evan swallowed hard. *Focus on your goals, man.* He was going to ride again. He'd never be lying in the dirt, facing a snake, and helpless as a baby again.

Libby unzipped her bag. "So, about the group you have coming in July..."

"The Wounded Patriots. I've decided to call it a retreat and maybe make it annual."

"Combat wounded?" Libby pulled out several thick bands of varying lengths, thicknesses, and colors. "Their stay coincides with your first goal, right?"

"Yep. I want to be in the saddle again by then. I'd like to rope off horseback by August, too."

"We'll have to see how therapy goes. I have a problem

with you taking a whole week off from therapy for the Wounded Patriot retreat." Libby gave him a sharp look.

"I'll continue my daily routine. I figure the others will benefit from seeing me keep after it."

Libby came closer, and it made his skin tingle. "I think the fact that you care to inspire others is great." She hesitated. "But not everyone can afford the therapies you have. I've worked with insurance limitations long enough to know that finances are a roadblock to many recovering veterans. They get basic P.T. But often, they must wait for it. They can't afford a private therapist in their home, and they rarely get animal-assisted therapies."

Evan scrubbed a hand along his jaw. "Equine, you mean?"

Libby nodded and pointed to her geriatric Golden Retriever, lumbering down the hall. "Or canine."

Evan stroked Pumpkin's head when she leaned against him. He hadn't known Libby had a dog at first. He was glad she'd asked permission to bring her to work.

"Canine therapy is brilliant. About the combat-wounded vets and their lack of resources...I've been thinking on that." Pumpkin was looking up at him with adoring eyes, and his heart turned to butter. "A few of the guys at our last meeting were discussing money problems. It changed my perspective. I'd like to do something, but I'm not sure what."

"I hope you come up with the idea you're searching for. So often helping others is a piece of the puzzle to our own heal-ing," Libby said. "How has your time with other veterans changed you?"

"For one thing, it made me more thankful for my family— and the whole ranching community." Hadn't there been parades and special events to honor him when he'd first come home? "They've all gotten behind me and helped in one way or another."

"They all love you." Libby shifted and began to pluck at a loose thread in the hem of her T-shirt.

"I heard about the amputee who committed suicide last year." At her terse nod, he went on, "Cody told me that he was a patient of yours. He said you took the guy's death hard. I'm sorry." Cody'd also let on that maybe Evan shouldn't dig into that wound but now that he had...

"How did Cody know?" She held up a hand. "Never mind. This is Apple Valley." Libby turned away with misty eyes.

He'd like to put an arm around her, but he wasn't sure how she'd take that.

Evan leaned in. "We have resources here. For starters, you're a licensed physical therapist with plenty of experience. The Three M has two empty bunkhouses off-season."

Libby's lashes brushed her cheeks before she lifted her face. "I've wanted to run an equine therapy program for a long time." Her cheeks colored.

The fact that Libby shared that with him warmed him. She was always closed off.

Although her tone was even, the passion in her eyes told him she cared very much about their topic. "Do you think therapies with animals and the out-of-doors are worth pursuing?

The studies I've read say that they offer tremendous healing advantages."

Evan nodded but that too-familiar feeling in his gut was back. "It helps to be in a more relaxed atmosphere. Being with people who have similar experiences and similar struggles… the nightmares, the…" His hands were getting clammy, and his throat tightened.

Libby put her hand on his forearm. "It's okay. I get it. Being outside helps everything."

Evan drew in a shaky breath and shook off the anxiety. "It always has for me."

"Some of my training and further education courses stated that water like rivers, streams, or natural ponds, as well as trees and animals, are therapeutic. The theory is that nature aids in mental and physical health. PTSD being what it is…"

Evan cleared his dry throat. He could use some fresh air right about now.

"Let's talk about it after we finish today's session." Libby kneeled in front of the little refrigerator against the back wall and pulled out a water bottle. She handed it to him.

After a throat-wetting swig, Evan wiped his mouth with the back of his hand. He scanned the motivational posters on the walls and took a fresh look at the equipment. "This room is a resource. We could have therapy sessions during the retreat week. I mean, my dad spent a fortune outfitting this room so we might as well share it." He pulled another gulp from the bottle. "There's a bike, rowing machine, weights, bench press, box jumps, sandbags… Just about everything you'd need. The wranglers and interns use the equipment during off-hours. One or more of them is always recovering from some sort of injury."

Libby's face split into a smile.

"You're catching my vision, aren't you?" Evan asked her with a smug grin.

She turned her full wattage on him, and his knee went weak.

"I am."

"We'll need gentle horses," Evan said. "Some of those guys have never ridden before."

"I'd love a chance to help out." She listed various professionals they might ask to volunteer for the week to make the most of the retreat.

The rest of his therapy session flew by. They made plans while they worked and talked about ways to modify the bunkhouse.

Libby's words of praise and validation earlier that morning kept Evan walking tall all day. He made a few calls, consulted Dad, and just like that, he'd become an event coordinator. The first Wounded Patriots Three M Ranch Retreat was on the calendar. The hardest part was choosing only three men for the trial week. They'd fill more slots when they were sure they knew what they were doing.

Libby had posed an insurance question Evan hadn't considered before. He'd need Dad to call Three M's attorney to answer a few legalities. On his way to the colt barn to find Dad, Evan stopped to pet the one-eyed tomcat. The half-feral ginger tabby flicked his tail but allowed Evan's attentions without clawing him for once.

The ranch's full-time farrier was bent over a buckskin's hind foot near the corral. Neal Fraser had worked for Grandpa Smokey since Evan and his brothers were a band of hooligans on the monkey bars at school. "Afternoon, Neal. Have you seen my dad?"

Neal lifted bloodshot eyes. Horseshoe nails poked from his lips like porcupine quills. He released the leg of the gelding and spoke around the nails. "Took the new three-year-old stud out to work cows. Can I help with something?"

Evan considered Neal. He knew horses. "I think you can." He told Neal his and Libby's plans. "I'll want half a dozen geldings to start. You'll know the type I'm looking for."

Neal nodded. "I got connections. Get back to ya soon as I have somethin' lined up. You got a crew to work them horses for you?"

"Not yet, but I'm thinking I can put a couple of the ranch interns on it."

"Six dead-broke nags." Neal spat a nail into his clawed hand, lifted the buckskin's hoof, and tapped a shoe in place with three well-placed strikes. "That's what you need." He pulled his lips back into a smile featuring a few tobacco-stained teeth resembling crooked old fence posts.

A dusty, black dually pick-up pulled around the long drive

with a livestock trailer behind it. The ranch dogs sprang from under their shady napping spots to harass its tires. If the driver was familiar, they'd duck their heads and wag their tails like they were ashamed of their behavior. If the driver was a stranger, they'd clamor an alarm until a human arrived.

Evan walked to the truck. His gait was gimpy, but it was better than even a few days ago. He was careful of his step in the middle of the pack of dogs. "Knock it off, Bones. Get back, Jed." Even so, two half-grown pups tussled behind him, and he hit the dirt like a load of manure. He landed on his butt with a crunching sound.

No. No. No.

He'd worked too hard to be taken down like a ranch rookie by a pack of cattle dogs. He groaned and flexed his limbs, trying to discover what was broken.

Dawson McClure, one of his many cousins, stepped out the truck and sauntered over. He didn't look too concerned.

Evan frowned up at him.

Dawson held out a hand with a mocking grin. "Got bucked off a bronc this morning. I dusted off and went back to work. You just fell on your butt. Get up ol' son."

Evan took the dirty, calloused hand and let Dawson pull him up.

"I heard something shatter when I landed." Evan passed a hand over each of his joints. His rear was sore and the hand he'd landed on was torn and bleeding. He wiped blood on his jeans.

Dawson snorted and pulled his hat lower, amusement in his eyes. "Check your back pocket, cuz."

Evan reached into his back pocket to find...pieces. He groaned. "Dang it. That was a new phone."

Dawson chuckled. "I brought a load of weanlings. Uncle Alex was supposed to be here." He looked around expectantly.

"Guess he forgot. I'd call the intern bunkhouse but—"

"No worries," Dawson said with a wink. "I'll unload the colts myself. Your dad said we could keep them in the field behind the tractor shed."

Evan nodded and left to nurse his injured pride in the house. He'd have to dig out his old phone.

"You going to the Cattlemen's Ball this year?"

Evan faced Dawson. "Why?"

"The association wants to recognize Grandpa Smokey and a couple of the older gents for their achievements. He wants all of Smokey's descendants present and accounted for. I only ask because we weren't sure—"

"That I'd be coming." Evan shot out his jaw. "Well, I am."

Dawson thumped his hat and walked back to his truck. He pulled on a pair of leather gloves and swung into the driver's seat. When the passenger side window came down, Evan took the cue and hobbled over. He was a little sorer than he'd admit.

"I was going to say we weren't sure about Nate coming."

Evan gave him a noncommittal shrug. Nate didn't come home anymore. He'd failed to show up for Cody's wedding, just gave the family some lame excuse by text.

Dawson shifted the truck into gear and pulled away,

leaving Evan coughing in a cloud of dust. One more reason Dawson wasn't his favorite cousin.

MOM GLIDED into the kitchen in fuzzy slippers. She wore linen pajamas and somehow managed to have every hair in place already this morning. Libby leaned against the counter with bleary eyes and bare feet.

"Morning, Lib. How'd you sleep?" Mom hid a yawn in the crook of her arm. She pulled two mugs from the cupboard and scooted Pumpkin from underfoot.

"fine." Libby lifted the lid on the coffee maker and slipped a filter inside. She measured out several scoops of dark roast, then scooped out another for good measure. She filled the machine with water from the tap and set the button to brew. "Grandma Rose still asleep?"

"Hmmm. Must be. Her dogs aren't up yet. They don't start their yapping until she comes out of her room."

Leaning against the counter, Libby rubbed her eyes and focused on the drip-drip-drip of the coffee. "I'm afraid I upset Grandma Rose last night."

Mom padded to the fridge and brought out the milk jug. "What do you mean?"

"She was here when I got a call from an equine therapy facility in Colorado. I'd applied last year but didn't get the position. There's another position opening at the end of summer, and the director called to encourage me to apply for it."

"You have a job." Mom set the milk on the counter next to the coffee pot.

"It's private pay and temporary. I don't have anything lined up after Evan. I need to start planning." Libby claimed the mug closest to her and splashed milk into it.

Mom poured steaming coffee into the other mug. "We'd assumed you were back in Apple Valley for good." She took a spoon and shut the silverware drawer hard. Pumpkin's ears shot up.

"That's what you told us." Mom dumped several heaping spoons of sugar into her mug and stirred like she was beating egg whites for a cake.

Libby laid a hand on Mom's arm. "Mom," she spoke in a gentle voice. "I know you'd always hoped all of us girls would settle in the valley. But the lack of opportunity—"

"Where opportunity is lacking, we make our own." Grandma Rose's gravelly morning voice interrupted Libby. Her fat corgi dogs barked at the door.

Libby walked to the French doors leading out to the garden and opened them to a sun-soaked lawn. Both corgis darted out. Pumpkin heaved her old bones up to follow them. The dogs startled a pair of robins pulling up breakfast worms. A magpie took flight and scolded them from the garden fence where he'd been pinching sweet peas off the vine.

"Pour me a cup of coffee please, Libby." Grandma Rose sat at the long pine table. She adjusted her hot pink robe around her chair like a queen.

Mom lifted the corner of her mouth and a brow as she doled portions of dog food into the bowls along the wall. She pushed Pumpkin's bowl further to one side, then she sat beside Grandma Rose. Libby pulled a third mug down, fixing Grandma's coffee the way she liked it, and joined them at the table. The dogs scratched at the glass-paned door to come inside as soon as she'd taken her chair. Libby sighed but rose and let the trio inside.

The corgis ran straight to their dishes, gobbled their kibble, and were settling at Gram's feet underneath the table before Libby had taken her first sip of coffee. Pumpkin lumbered to her dish, sniffed, and gave Libby a reproachful look.

"Go on, eat your breakfast, Pumpkin. You're too picky for a dog. Especially a rescue," Mom put her foot down when it came to feeding Pumpkin treats and soft food. "Bad for her teeth," she'd claimed.

Libby gave an I'm-sorry-girl look to her dog. "Go on, eat up."

Resigned, Pumpkin stretched out in front of the dish. She ate one piece of kibble at a time as if she were a child forced to eat broccoli.

Gram leaned sideways in her chair and rooted around in her robe pocket. She pulled out a wad of used Kleenex and tossed it on the table, then reached back inside the pocket. She pulled out her dentures, examined them, polished them with the sleeve of her robe, then popped them into her mouth. She fished around in the pocket again, brought out her signature orange lipstick, and applied a thick coat to her lips.

Mom met Libby's eyes and shook her head the tiniest bit, but she was fighting back a smile, too.

"Now," Grandma Rose sounded business-like as she pulled her mug close, took a sip, wrinkled her nose, and pushed it toward Libby. "More sugar, please." There was an orange lip print on the rim.

Libby retrieved the sugar bowl, and when they all had their coffee the way they liked, the dogs were settled, and the caffeine had started to kick in, Gram cleared her throat.

"You know Molly took her inheritance when she came back to live in Apple Valley."

Libby nodded. She refrained from sneaking a peak at her watch. She had to get to the Three M for Evan's therapy session. Hopefully, Gram wasn't working up to a long lecture on family responsibility. She never got tired of inspiring "her ladies" to stay rooted in Apple Valley. She kept forgetting that small towns meant small opportunities. Not that Libby didn't want to live here. She did.

But she wasn't going to waste six years of college.

"Molly wanted your grandfather's art studio for her silver-smithing. Josie said at Christmas she'd like to have the old art gallery I own on the same block. She means to have a boutique there when she finally settles down." Gram lifted a brow, but it didn't have the effect she was going for since she hadn't drawn them on yet that morning.

Mom hugged her coffee mug to her chest. "Imagine what it would be like to have all of us together again."

Libby gave her a smile despite a twinge of guilt. How

could she stay? There was precious little need for another physical therapist in a town this small. She'd already inquired at the clinic, but they used such outdated equipment. Besides, they couldn't afford to pay her what she was used to even if they had a position available. Which they didn't.

Grandma Rose dipped into her pocket again and brought out another tissue, a little less used than the others. "You have never been clear about which property you would like. Before he passed on, your grandfather made provision for each of you girls to own real estate in Apple Valley." She dabbed at her eyes. "It was his—our—wish, to see our daughters and their children well-settled."

"I know, Gram." Libby put her hand over Grams' gnarled knuckles. "But this little town doesn't need me."

"Phooey," she said in a gruff voice. "I was thinking you'd like the sixty-five acres and the old farmhouse."

"But…I thought that was meant for Aunt Olivia." The property was run down, but pure gold for its location. Libby had never dreamed of being offered her grandparent's first homestead. She'd always assumed it would go to Mom's older sister since Mom had this farm.

"Olivia doesn't want it. Besides, she isn't coming back to Apple Valley, and we don't want any of the properties sold to outsiders."

"But the house on that property is already occupied."

"Old Lefty Hanson has been living there for a dozen years, which is why the house is so run down." Mom's voice dripped disapproval, as it always did when discussing the man

Grandpa had moved into the house to live rent-free. "The old squatter."

Gram brushed Mom's words aside. "Your daddy felt sorry for him. They were in Vietnam together and...well, you already know all of this." She locked eyes with Libby over the rim of her cup. "I'm sure Lefty can be persuaded to share the house."

"Share the house?" Mom's voice rose and the indignant note matched the one inside Libby's head.

Share a house with that raggedy old man? Ridiculous. She nearly laughed but the glint in Gram's eyes prevented her from that mistake. Grandpa had paid the electricity bill and water for the property while he was alive. As far as she knew, Grandma Rose had continued the charity all these years.

"Gram, as sweet as the sentiment is—and I do appreciate it," Libby added, seeing storm clouds brewing,"even if the house were in good condition and Lefty weren't living there, I still couldn't move in. I need an income."

"Something will come along," Gram said in a too-breezy tone. The set of her chin spoke of determination.

"I appreciate the offer, but I don't think ousting an old veteran from his home will do much to promote me as a therapist dedicated to helping veterans." Libby ran a hand through her tangled curls. "I'd better jump in the shower. I'll be late to work."

"Wait." Mom held her hand up. "Libby, your dream is combing physical therapy with animal therapy for your clients, right?"

"Yes. But I don't have the credentials for working with PTSD yet. I'd need to take more classes."

"The old homestead would make a great equine facility." Mom gave her a shrewd look. She and Gram had been communicating in code with their eyes. Libby was thrust back to her teenage years when she and her sisters were outmatched by them more often than not.

Libby peered at her watch. "You're the one who brought up Lefty Hanson. I can't kick him out, and I sure can't live with him."

"Just promise me you won't write the idea off completely. We'll pray for a solution." Gram stood. "I've decided that's the inheritance you're getting. What you choose to do with it is up to you." She puffed her chest like a broody hen.

What on earth was she going to do with a crumbling old farmhouse and a geriatric roommate? She pictured the horror in Lefty's face when he swung open the squeaky door to her, surrounded by moving boxes, on the front porch.

She snorted into her coffee cup.

EVAN WIPED his sweaty brow with the hem of his tank top. Libby had been preoccupied during their therapy session. He'd hoped to discuss the retreat, but she'd only given him a stern look and informed him that he'd miscounted his muscle-up reps when he brought it up.

"You have at least three more to do." She didn't look at him. She was staring out the window.

"What's caught your eye out there?" Evan asked. He reached for the muscle-up bar and counted out three more even though he'd only missed one, and he'd done that just to see if Libby was paying attention to him.

"Nothing," she said on a sigh. Which meant it *was* something.

Stiff and sore as he was from falling yesterday, he hadn't held back on his morning workout. He stifled a groan as he sat on the bench. Pumpkin eyed him from where she lay, then got up with a whine and tail wag. She pushed her graying muzzle into his hand and then put her paw in his lap.

"You are an astute lady, Pumpkin." He ruffled the thick golden mane around her neck and then smoothed the fluff around her ears. She licked him in reply.

Dogs always knew.

"What's that?" Libby asked when a scuffle of shoes in the hallway drew her attention.

Evan waved to Theo, who peeked from the hall with only his eyes and nose visible. "Hey, buddy."

"Hey, Uncle Evan." Theo ventured in but kept his eyes on Libby. The children had strict instructions from Papa Alex not to bother them during therapy.

"It's okay, Theo. We're finished for the day." Libby still had a faraway look in her eye.

"I wanted to pet Pumpkin." Theo reached his little hand out, and the dog licked it with enthusiasm.

Evan laughed. "I think you'd better wash the lunch off your hands before Mrs. M catches you leaving handprints on her walls again."

Theo cocked his hip. "She ain't here. She went to visit her sister in Ellensburg for the night. Salty is cooking for the family and the bunkhouse."

Evan caught Libby's eye. "You know what that means, don't you?"

"No clue," she replied. She held her arms open for Theo. He stepped inside her hug with a lopsided smile. She kissed the top of his head.

Theo stepped back, wiping smears of peanut butter on his jeans. "It means we're gonna have barbecue and baked beans."

"If your smile is anything to go by, I'd say this is good news." She scrubbed at a jelly stain Theo had left on her T-shirt.

Theo bobbed his head. "Salty is a great cooker."

"From time to time he cooks for us, along with the cowboys and interns," Evan explained.

"I remember. He managed the huge barbecue at Molly and Cody's wedding." Libby licked her thumb and took a swipe at a smudge on Theo's chin.

Evan's heart turned to mashed potatoes at the tender gesture. "You're welcome to come for dinner. Bring your mom and grandmother. Grandpa Smokey loves to talk old times with Rowdy Rosey."

Theo sat cross-legged on the floor next to Pumpkin. The dog snuffled his ears, and he giggled. Evan smiled but caught his breath when he glanced at Libby and read the sweetness in her expression. Why wasn't she married with a couple of kids? She obviously liked them.

"I'll call later and let you know if we're coming by," Libby said. She knelt in front of Theo. "Think you can keep an eye on Pumpkin for me? I'd like to run up and see your mama and baby Rose." She stood and then frowned. "Theo, why aren't you at school?"

"I had a doctor appointment this morning. Dad took me. Mom said I get to stay home the rest of the day as long as I promise to muck out my pony's stall."

"Have you done it?" Evan asked.

Theo's eyes grew wide. He shook his head. "Not yet."

"If you keep an eye on Pumpkin, I'll walk out to the barn with you so I can visit Emmet."

"You gonna ride that ol' horse again?"

"Not yet." Libby crossed her arms and tipped a bossy brow.

Evan shrugged. "Maybe I'll just let him run in the round pen for a while. No harm in that."

"If I catch you on the back of a horse, Evan McClure, you'll have more to worry about than—"

"Hey now." Evan stopped her. "There are tender ears present. Besides, there's no call for threats. Emmet's a kind old soul."

Libby gave him a warning glare on her way out the door. "I'm going upstairs to see Molly." She swiveled around. "Theo, please make sure your uncle doesn't do anything stupid."

Theo gaped at her, turned his head to Evan, then back to Libby. "I don't want that 'sponsibility."

Libby cracked a smile. "You're right, kiddo. Keeping your uncle out of trouble is too much to ask." She speared a glance at Evan, then gave Theo a warm look. "I'll come back down in a bit, and then you can go do your chores, okay?"

"Okay, Aunt Libby. Pumpkin and me will watch *Curious George* cartoons."

"Remember not to let Papa Alex or Grandpa Smokey find you allowing the dog on the couch, buddy." Evan said. "You'll catch heck."

When Evan was sure Libby was out of earshot, he grunted and stood. Maybe he'd overdone it today. This morning he'd been bruised all over his bottom half. "I'll go change, then we can head to the barn."

Theo tugged on Pumpkin's collar. "Holler when you're ready. Pumpkin's favorite episode is up next."

Evan raised his brows. "Do tell. How often does this dog watch *Curious George*?"

"Whenever she can."

Theo walked beside the retriever down the hall toward the great room. Pumpkin's nails clack-clacked on the wood. Evan picked up his towel, tossed it in the hamper, and turned off the lights on his way out. Spending some time with Emmet would improve his mood.

Staying positive was a struggle when everything hurt— including his pride. It was definitely sore after the swing in

Libby's attitude toward him. Her mind was elsewhere today. There was something else, too. He just couldn't quite name it. Maybe she'd met someone? She was bound to sooner or later. She was a great…therapist.

From now on, he'd focus on getting back in the saddle and quit allowing himself to get sidetracked by a pretty face. His ego was still too fragile to attempt to win over any woman, especially Libby Halverson.

Chapter 4

ALL KINDS OF PAIN

L ibby crossed her arms behind her head on the twin bed she'd had since she was fifteen. With her bedroom window cracked, the pond songs of croaking frogs and violin-playing crickets lulled her to a pleasant, relaxed state. She fluffed her pillow and settled in to ponder what she and Evan had discussed over a finger-licking rack of beef ribs at dinner. He'd been distant at the beginning of the evening but after a good meal that included plenty of banter at the family table, they'd all been feeling chummy by the end.

She'd come home to Apple Valley to be near her family. Being homesick and lonely had spurred her return when her last contract ended. Traveling for work was lucrative, but she'd had about as many lonely nights in temporary lodgings with Netflix and take-out as she could stand. Besides, she missed horses. And men in boots and wrangler jeans who opened doors for women and said things like, "yes, ma'am."

She was home now, for however long. Libby whispered her prayers and drifted off.

The next morning, she slept through her alarm. She rushed through brushing her teeth, skipped doing her hair, and concluded she'd have to do without coffee.

Leaving the house without her morning brew might not have been the best course of action. A slow-moving tractor in the road had cost her more time. Then an old pick-up truck was parked in her regular spot near the side of the main house. That required her to find another place to park out of the way of the constant flow of ranch trucks and trailers. By the time she reached the ranch house, she was in a mood.

Without a caffeine fix—as soon as possible—her attitude was going to get her into trouble.

She let herself in around the back entrance. The downstairs kitchen was quiet but the tromping of boots on the wooden floors upstairs indicated it was business as usual for the McClures. Mrs. M greeted her and started a pot of coffee. Leaning against the counter, Libby answered emails on her phone while she waited. When the coffee pot beeped, she filled a mug with steaming dark roast, a generous glug of vanilla creamer, and headed to the gym to meet Evan for their therapy session.

On her way down the hall her phone pinged a text from Molly. Annoyance tightened her neck muscles when she read the message. What she found when she got to the gym did not improve her mood.

Libby set her mug on the windowsill and stood in front of Evan with her arms crossed and a glower in place.

He didn't look up.

She cleared her throat and frowned.

Still nothing.

She'd have to work on her mean face. According to Molly's tattletale text, he'd been on the stationary bike for an hour. "You're in trouble, Evan McClure." Libby unplugged the bike and glared.

"Hey!"

He glared back as the machine died beneath him.

"Are you trying to undo the work we've done? Is your pride worth more than your progress? Or maybe you're trying to put me out of a job?"

Evan mopped sweat from his face with his T-shirt and squinted up at her. "My pride and my butt took a tumble yesterday. I'm tryin' to make faster progress so I can move on to saddle work. I need to pull my weight around here."

Libby averted her eyes from Evan's six pack abs—toasted tan from time spent poolside—and doubled up efforts at giving him dirty looks. "Your progress reflects my professional abilities. I have to give a weekly account to your surgeon. If you injure yourself, you're setting us both back." She tossed him a towel from the shelf.

Evan winced but caught the towel and wiped his hands.

Libby settled on a bench and glared harder.

He took a long drink from the water bottle in the bike's cup holder. He was being deliberately slow.

Libby crossed her legs and tapped her finger on the bench.

Evan fixed an exaggerated hound dog expression on her and said, "I'm sorry."

She lifted her chin high. "I doubt it."

Swinging his leg over the stationary bike, he lost his balance when his prosthetic hit the bar. He grabbed for the handles of the machine.

Libby shot up and pushed her weight against his side to keep him from falling. His body radiated sticky heat and sweaty effort. He was quivering with overexertion.

"Look at you, for crying out loud." She chastised him to cover her worry. Or maybe to cover her attraction. Evan was a big male with all the clichéd attractive features of a heart-throb movie star. This job would be easier if Evan were a mean, nasty man. "You look like a spooked wild stallion."

He steadied himself with a heavy arm slung across her shoulder. She could swear he—no. Did he? Yes. Evan had sniffed her hair. Libby tilted her head up and caught her breath. His eyes were so…hungry.

"Are you okay, cowboy? You overdid it today. You probably swam laps before I came too, huh?" The pheromones in the air befuddled her brain and told her lies. This attraction was old news. She'd outgrown it, she reminded herself with a stern tone inside her head.

She attempted a feeble smile and pushed Evan's chest away from her shoulder.

Evan moved away from her hand. "Sorry."

But she'd caught a glimpse of his white, thinned lips before he turned aside.

"You're in pain," she accused him. She wanted to retract the words. Evan was her patient, not a child.

He nodded then slumped his shoulders in defeat.

Libby helped him sit on the bench along the wall. He was heavy. Panting, she blew hair out of her eyes and tightened her ponytail, then bent to rest her hands on her knees. "Okay, out with it." Clearly, something had happened.

"I guess I fell harder than I thought."

"You fell?"

Evan clenched his eyes. "Yesterday."

"What hurts? Is it your implant site?"

He shook his head. "No. My hip." He rubbed the spot.

"Your hip hurts so you decided to go ahead and ride the stationary bike all morning? Outrageous. I mean, really, of all the—"

"Stop, please. I already know it was stupid."

"Then why on earth would you... Never mind." She snapped her mouth shut.

Evan gave her an injured look.

Sighing, Libby got eye-to-eye with Evan. "I'm going to focus on the fact that you're a man who is determined and resilient. Those qualities will help us reach your goals. But listen." She put a hand on his shoulder and tried to ignore the sizzle. "You need to go in for an x-ray now. You know that, right?"

Evan folded his hands on his chest and used his ab muscles

to lower himself flat along the narrow bench. He blew out a heavy breath. "Okay."

Evan was silent during the drive to the clinic. He stared out the window at the blur of hay fields and cattle. He didn't react when Libby swerved to avoid a slinking coyote in the road. At the clinic, his jaw was set, his lips pressed tight. Was he mad at her? More likely scared. His future was tied up in healing from surgery, not requiring another one.

Once the X-ray was done, read, and discussed, Libby gathered their things. "That's a relief. But there's no way you can start having time in the saddle until the inflammation in that hip is down."

The ride back to the Three M was less tense but no less quiet. Libby settled Evan in the great room with an icepack, and Mrs. Mulligan brought him a glass of lemonade. Frozen raspberries bobbed on the surface and a sprig of mint drowned underneath, lodged between the ice cubes. Evan fished out the mint and tossed it on the side table. He stared out the large picture window.

They sat in cowhide-covered chairs with the glassy eyes of mounted elk and deer staring at them from the walls. A ceiling fan wafted a gentle breeze over their heads. Libby squirmed in her chair and sipped the lemonade Mrs. Mulligan had served her. The woman was a gem, but Evan hadn't thanked her.

Libby leaned forward with her arms across her knees. "Evan, the x-ray showed good news. The hip was only bruised." Thank goodness. But it was a setback.

Evan turned a half smile her way then resumed staring out the window.

There were miles of bright green fields, some dotted with cattle, some with horses. The orchards lay beyond the view from this angle. A Goldfinch landed on the other side of the window and peered in, meeting Libby's eyes with his little black beads.

Libby picked at her fingernails and peeked at Evan. "I'm sorry."

Evan faced her with a question in the lift of his brow.

"I spoke to you in a demeaning tone this morning."

Evan shrugged. "You always were bossy." The glint of humor in his eye was reassuring.

"I don't want to squash your drive to be successful."

Evan slid his lemonade glass in circles on the table between their chairs. "You were busy traveling for work the past couple of years. Helping people." He inclined his head toward her as if he wanted her to affirm his statement.

She nodded.

"Meantime, I was sitting in a wheelchair, feeling sorry for myself. I cannot go back to being that pitiful man."

So. That was it. He'd come out of the valley of the shadow of death and was afraid of sliding down that slope again.

"You were dealing with a lot."

He gave a soft, mocking snort. "At least I'm alive." Pain dulled his eyes. "They treated me like a hero when I finally got back to Apple Valley. Had a parade and—"

"You are a hero." It wasn't like she hadn't been down this

road before. Many veterans dealt with survivor's guilt and PTSD. But seeing Evan like this after he'd always been bigger than life was unsettling. How perverse that so much had been stolen from this man she'd grown up secretly—or maybe not so secretly—admiring. Besides, just now he reminded her of Luke before he retreated into depression.

That frightened her.

Evan swiped his huge hand over his face. "I'm no hero. Dave Frank was a hero. But he didn't get a parade," Evan's voice cracked. "He got a body bag."

Libby rested her hand over the top of Evan's. Dave must be his friend, the one who didn't make it home. Evan didn't pull away, so she held his hand and squeezed. "We don't get to choose who survives a war. But you can choose to live life well for Dave and the others who died. Don't throw away the gift of life." Her chin wobbled and tears thickened her throat. "God allowed you to survive something catastrophic…all things work together for the good of those who love Him and are called according to His purposes. You remember that verse?"

With a wavering smile, Evan squeezed her hand back. "Dave quoted that once or twice. Mostly whenever we started missing home and our girls." A flash of pain flitted over his features. "Angela's letters kept me going in that sweltering desert." He sat straighter. "But I understand why she broke things off. Who wants a man with only one leg, right?"

Libby clenched her jaw for a moment before answering. "Her loss. Everyone was so relieved that you came home alive.

This town loves its own. You have shined brighter than most, so it has loved you more."

"Not shining anymore though, am I?"

Libby smiled and knew her heart was in her eyes but let him see it anyway. "I expect a return to blinding brilliance soon."

Evan smiled sadly and took his hand back. "That Evan is long gone."

"Evan-two-point-oh, then. You're always going to be a star, no matter what. It's who you are." She slapped his intact leg. "Rest up. I'm coming back at you tomorrow."

"The doctor said—"

"We'll only do what's allowed. But we won't quit."

"We?" Evan cocked an eyebrow.

"Yes, we. You aren't doing this alone. Apple Valley wants you back, Superman."

"And you?"

"If you succeed, I succeed." Libby swallowed the lump in her throat.

It wasn't a lie.

LATE AFTERNOON SUN evaporated the water droplets on Evan's shoulders. He basked in the warmth as he sat drip-drying on the pool's edge. Sunlight reflected on the surface of the water, little dancing rays. He slowed his breath after the exertion of timed laps and listened to his heart slow its rhythm.

Mrs. M would call them all to dinner soon, but he closed his eyes anyway. His hip ached with fury. At least the purple bruises on his lower half were fading into ugly yellow and green.

"Hey, wake-up!" Theo's freckled nose was two inches from Evan's unsuspecting face.

Evan bolted upright. "Buddy, don't ever do that to an ex-soldier." His voice was faint and shaky. The booming in his chest was nearly as loud as the ringing in his ears.

Theo stumbled back but smiled with a look that said he trusted Evan completely, even if Evan did jump out of his skin occasionally.

"Mom says you need to get dressed and come to the table."

Evan smiled at the way Theo referred to Molly as his mother without hesitation. The Bible verse Dad quoted often came to mind—the one about love covering a multitude of sins —yeah. That. There was another verse Libby had suggested too, one about all things working together for good. He'd believed for years that God had thrown him off like an ornery bronc. The notion took hold the day he'd gotten blown up. But God wasn't a cherry-picker, was He? Grandma McClure used to say that God didn't have favorites, but sometimes Evan wondered.

Theo yanked on Evan's hand. "Come on! Mom's going to say you don't get dessert if you're late to supper."

"Oh, no." Evan kept his face straight, although he wanted to chuckle. "No dessert?" He locked his prosthetic in place, pocketed the tool, and allowed Theo to think he'd pulled Evan's big body up.

Theo strained and pulled a dramatic face as he hauled on Evan's arm. "When are you going to get married like Dad did? And how come Papa Alex didn't get married?" Theo frowned up at him.

Honest questions deserved honest answers. "Your grandfather used to be married a long time ago."

"To your mom?"

Evan nodded and tightened his hold on Theo's hand. "Yes."

"Did she die like Great-Gramma?"

"No. She went to live in the city. Life on a ranch is pretty hard, and some folks don't get along here."

"Oh." Theo swiped a finger under his nose. "Is that why you don't have a wife?"

"That's a longer story. Just like living on a cattle ranch doesn't suit some folks, marrying a man with only one leg doesn't suit most ladies."

Theo nodded. "'Cause they like to dance, huh?"

"Exactly." Evan met Theo's eyes with a rueful smile. "Now, run to the table before you're late. And tell your mom I'll be down after I change."

"Okay, but hurry," Theo implored.

Now that he'd decided to take his life back, he'd like someone to share it with. But the look on Angela's face when the nurse in the rehabilitation center had thrown back the sheet covering his stump... That had burned a hole in his memory and his heart. He never wanted to see that look again.

Every guy needed to feel like he was a little bit dangerous. Even a guy in a wheelchair. Seeing pity in a woman's eyes killed that feeling. Flirting with Libby was one thing, risking his reawakening manhood was another. He ground his molars.

"Come on," Theo hollered. He'd stopped to examine something crawling on the ground.

Evan chuckled. "I told you to go ahead. You're almost as bossy as your Aunt Libby."

Theo's head popped up. "Aunt Libby is nice. She don't boss me."

"Doesn't. Libby doesn't boss you." Evan corrected him.

"Well, she doesn't. She's pretty." Theo pointed at Evan's chest. "You like her."

"You can stop that right now. Don't you go around spreading scandal." He winked and gave Theo a playful swat. "We have to play it cool."

Theo peered up at him.

"Your dad hasn't taught you a thing about women, has he?"

"They make good moms. And Dad said I should be nice to sisters."

"Guess I'm wrong. Your dad about covered it all." Evan roughed Theo's close-cropped hair and gave way to the smile tugging at his mouth.

Theo shoved the stink bug he'd found in the dirt into his pocket.

Evan would give anything for some of Theo's goodness

and innocence. But he was jaded. Angela dumping him at his lowest point probably sealed the deal. Theo's biological mom had done the same thing to him though, and he didn't let it drag him down. He was just a kid, but kids were basic. And didn't the Bible say to have faith like a child? Maybe he should let Theo inspire him, rather than feeling he needed to set the example just because he'd been on the globe longer.

Down syndrome had its upsides. Theo believed the best of everyone he met.

Evan and Theo hustled inside when Molly used the intercom system to remind them dinner was getting cold. The annoyance in her voice was detectable over the speaker. Too many late nights with a teething baby had soured her disposition lately.

Evan parted ways with Theo and headed upstairs to change. He pulled a black T-shirt with the Three M brand on it from the closet and tugged it on. He skinned on an old pair of Wranglers. His sneakers squeaked on the hallway floor as he hurried to dinner.

Back downstairs all conversation around the long table stopped when he walked in. Molly lowered her eyes and began to fuss with baby Rose's bib. He'd expected her to give him the business for holding up their meal. Dad, intent on cutting Theo's steak, only glanced up. Cody was the only one who would meet his eyes, but they were full of...sorrow? Compassion? He couldn't quite read them. They'd all gotten pretty good at hiding their feelings around him. He supposed they'd had to.

Evan pressed his lips together. Should he just ask? Or maybe leave it be? Whatever it was it could wait, he was hungry. Dad passed him the platter of rib-eye steaks, and Bella plopped a baked potato on his plate.

"Here ya go, Uncle Evan. Eat up." She passed him the butter.

He cut a generous slab, opened the potato's jacket, slid the butter over the steamy insides and mashed it with green onions and liberal shakes of salt and pepper. He picked up his fork. All the adults were staring at him.

"Eh...do I want to know?"

"Don't forget your greens." Molly slid a glass salad bowl within his reach.

Everyone's eyes returned to their plates.

Evan peppered his steak, poured a glass of milk, asked Dad to pass the carrots. When he'd loaded his plate, he placed his napkin in his lap and sat back. "Did someone say grace?"

"I did," Bella said. "I said it for you, too."

"Thank you." He'd get indigestion if the tension in the room got any thicker. But his questions would have to wait until the kids went upstairs for the night.

After they'd eaten, including pie and ice cream for dessert, Cody sent Bella and Theo upstairs to get ready for bed.

Mrs. M cleared the table. She wouldn't meet Evan's eyes when he thanked her.

"She's a good cook," Cody said in a conversational tone as Mrs. M left the room.

Evan cocked a brow in his brother's direction.

"She is," Molly agreed. "The chili she made last night was terrific. The grilled onions and mushrooms topping the steaks were a nice touch tonight."

"The blue cheese was a treat," Dad said.

Evan eyed each one in turn. Yep. There was definitely something going on and it seemed everyone but him knew what it was. He tapped a finger on the table. Mrs. M was a reliable gossip if a person knew the right way to ask her a question.

"I'll just go check on the kids." Molly settled baby Rose in Cody's arms and retreated from the dining room.

"Let me have my granddaughter, hey? I haven't held her all day." Dad leaned forward with his arms out.

Evan pushed out of his chair and excused himself. He grimaced at the twinge in his sore hip and used the chair to keep his balance. Once his prosthetic was underneath him, he left the room with as much dignity as he could muster. It was time to find Mrs. M, and he knew just where to look.

Tomorrow was sweet roll day. Evan inhaled the yeasty scent of dough rising in a bowl in preparation on the counter. Warm vanilla scented the air over another bowl. The world could end tomorrow, but with Mrs. M managing them, they'd eat well before they died.

Evan found her at the desk in her office off the kitchen, head bent over a list. He cleared his throat from the doorway.

She startled and swiveled in her chair.

Evan held her eyes until hers lowered to fiddle with the pen in her lap. "Mrs. M..." Shortening her name usually softened her. "I was wondering if there might be something going on, something I should know about?" He did his level best to keep his voice free of the wheedling tone all women were wired to resist.

Mrs. M gave him a nervous smile, dropped her pen, and bent to retrieve it. Then she began to arrange her desk. "I... what do you mean? Is there something you wanted, or..."

She was going to make this difficult.

Evan stepped inside the small room and leaned against her desk. "We can do this the hard way, or we can do this the easy way. You know something I don't. It feels like something I should know."

"Oh. I'm not sure I should be the one to..." She wrung her hands. Mrs. M had been a very pretty woman once upon a time. Before her dirtbag husband left her with a houseful of kids and a mortgage in arrears. She'd made a nice addition to the Three M, and best of all, she was soft where he was concerned.

Evan summoned a good amount of charm and fixed a boyish smile across his face. This tactic had worked since he was a small child, but he was rusty. He gauged her response and widened his eyes like a new calf.

She was crumbling.

"Out with it," he coaxed her.

Chapter 5

COWBOYS AND BABES

The back entrance of the Three M ranch house was locked, with no sign of life. Libby lifted the silver knocker on the solid cherry-wood front door. The house was rustic, but grand. The front door had been carved in minute detail with galloping wild horses at least a century past. The back entrance was locked, with no sign of life.

Pumpkin cocked her head and lifted her ears when the yapping poodles sounded on the other side of the door. Libby set her tote on one of the wooden benches, carved and painted with cacti, Road Runners, and the Three M cattle brand.

She bent to examine a Painted Lady butterfly resting on one of the enormous potted plants on either side of the door. White flowers bloomed in the center of each pot. Their sweet perfume a draw for pollinators. Libby remembered Grandpa Cameron's nature study lessons during long summer breaks from school.

At last, a creaky hinge moaned, the door opened, and a wisp of cool air kissed her face from inside.

Bella and Theo appeared in the entryway. The birds in nearby trees burst into flight when Pinky and Daisy rushed out. Pumpkin ignored them and plopped down in a shady corner near a bench, having chosen her spot for the morning.

Libby kneeled and gave each poodle a pat. "Hello, ankle biters." The dogs kissed her face. "Yuck." She stood and wiped her chin dry. "Those rascals need breath mints." Looking down, she pretended to speak to Bella's dog. "Pinky, how is your pet girl today? Daisy, has your pet boy kept your treat dish full?"

Bella rolled her eyes, entirely too mature for this game, but Theo doubled over, laughing.

"Where's your uncle, kiddos?"

"He's in the pool again. Mom says he's going to prune up if he doesn't stop." Bella scooped Pinky up and buried her nose in the dog's curly topknot.

Libby peered around the door. "Where's your mom?"

"Feeding baby Rose in the nursery," Theo said. He picked up Daisy, who squirmed and managed to untie one of her navy-blue ear ribbons with her sharp little teeth. Theo offered the unruly dog to Libby.

"No thanks, Daisy. I've had enough doggie kisses." She hefted her bag over her shoulder and pulled her sticky shirt away from her skin. The heat was abusive this morning. It would probably be cool again tomorrow. Changeable weather was a Pacific Northwest trait.

"Watch out for Uncle Evan's attitude today," Bella warned her.

"Oh?"

Theo shot Bella a sharp look. "He's sad."

"He's crabby," Bella insisted. "Dad says to keep clear of him for a few days because he has a lot on his mind." Bella put Pinky down and shoved her hands inside her pockets in a pout. "He's usually fun."

"Don't worry. Everyone has bad days occasionally. I'm sure he'll be in a better mood tomorrow." Much like the weather.

"I hope so," Theo said. "But I heard Mom say his heart was broke."

Libby lifted Theo's chin with a gentle finger. "What do you mean?"

Theo gave an unhelpful shrug.

She turned to Bella and quizzed her with an eyebrow.

Bella motioned Libby to come closer and spoke low. "The lady who was supposed to marry him a long time ago is marrying somebody else."

The air in Libby's lungs seemed to settle to the bottom like sand. "Lady, huh? Poor Evan."

"Exactly," Bella said out of the side of her mouth.

"You said he's in the pool?" Libby asked.

Both children nodded solemnly.

"Thanks, guys."

Inside the empty work-out room., Libby tossed her bag in a corner. If Angela was getting married and Evan knew, he was probably in a sorry state of mind. Should she push him to complete therapy today or give him a break? How would he react to physical pain considering his emotional pain? She wandered toward the door leading to the pool.

Evan might not appreciate her making a big deal out of Angela's engagement.

In the hallway, she examined her hair and face in the mirror. She should have applied a little tinted sunscreen at least. She'd just have to make friends with her freckles, they were here to stay, and the sun only made more. Glancing into the mirror one more time, she got close and whispered, "Your job is to see that Evan stays on his therapy schedule and meets his goals. Nothing more." She shook her finger at her reflection. "I mean it."

Potted lemon and lime trees stood in alternating patterns on one side of the fence enclosing the pool area. Nestled in a corner, a sunshade covered a glass table, inviting her to sit and escape the sun. She did have those freckles to worry about, after all.

A pitcher of lemonade dripped condensation on a tray next to crystal glasses. They were turned upside down. Probably to keep insects out. A bowl of sugared lemon slices and raspberries sat beside a dish of mint sprigs. The McClures might be rough cowboys, but they sure did get spoiled by Mrs. Mulligan.

Libby sat, sighed in gratitude, and fixed a fancy glass of lemonade. It was hot enough to fry eggs on the pavement.

Libby drained half her glass, then stood in a patch of shade to watch Evan swim and consider her next move.

Bronzed shoulders plowed through the water. Evan's upper body rippled with bulky muscle. Liquid beads rolled down his back as he porpoised from one end of the pool to the other. His biceps and forearms were remarkable. He'd had to bear all his weight on them for years, so they would be.

Libby tore her eyes from Evan's body and drifted back to the table. She sat under the shade and poured another glass of lemonade for herself, and one for Evan. She garnished Evan's glass with a sugared lemon slice but thought better of the sprig of mint. He always picked it out. She refreshed the ice in her glass and sat back to wait. This wasn't going to be Evan's finest hour if the set of his jaw was anything to go by.

Keeping her eyes averted from the pool, she pondered the blue sky and small puffs of clouds. They floated haphazardly, like balloons released for a special occasion. She was just trying to make out the shape of the one above the nearest barn when she spied Bella and Theo zooming past, poodles running ahead, Pumpkin lagging behind. An impulse to smile was stopped short by a pucker after biting a bit of lemon pulp.

The dogs reminded her of a time she'd seen Cody at the Apple Valley rodeo. He'd been toting one of the poodles on the back of a fancy, blue roan gelding. She'd noted a snicker here and there, but more often, Cody got a nod of respect. He didn't care what anybody thought. Women of all ages had swooned over him and that dog, but his heart belonged to Molly. That was plain enough for anybody to see.

It wouldn't be a half-bad feeling to have a handsome cowboy stuck like glue to Libby.

She'd envied Molly's family life since coming home to Apple Valley. She'd even had a ridiculous dream that she and Evan were at an altar, exchanging vows of till death do us part. The dream still noodled around in her brain and caused her cheeks to feel sunburned.

"What are you thinking about?" Evan called from the side of the pool. He watched her while he toweled his hair. The sun caught his flexed lats and the manly shadow on his jaw.

"Your brother," Libby answered.

Evan's brows rose.

"It cracks me up the way he carries those poodles horseback sometimes." Libby debated bringing up the news about Angela's engagement. Why rub dirt into the wound? Most likely he didn't want to talk about it, especially with her. "I poured you some lemonade."

Evan pushed his weight up with his forearms and pulled his legs out of the water. He dried his stump and implant carefully, then reached for his prosthetic and screwed it on. His movements were graceful.

Libby checked his expression for signs of discomfort or pain. His hip still bothered him if she read his body language right, but it seemed the implant had healed. With the scab so recently torn off his wounded heart, she was glad he hadn't done more damage to himself when he'd fallen.

Evan lowered himself into the chair opposite her. He finger-combed his wet hair back, lifted arms showcasing bulging biceps. He was every bit as poster worthy as he'd ever been.

Libby sipped her lemonade to wet her dry mouth. She set the tall glass on the table and absently wiped away condensation from the sides.

Evan stared at her with an inscrutable expression.

She gave a nervous little cough. "Want to talk about it?"

Evan snorted, picked the sugared lemon slice from the lip of his glass, and flung it on the table. "No." He sighed "Maybe."

"You might feel better."

"I don't really feel bad, I'm just…disappointed."

Libby licked a bit of sugar from her finger. "Oh?" Disappointment? That was unexpected.

"I was crushed when Angela said she couldn't love me anymore. I wasn't the man she'd waited for. But after a long while, I realized I was more disappointed in myself for not catching her character sooner. I'd promised to give her my future and I meant it. I still would have, even knowing how she felt about me."

Libby focused on her lemonade.

"Have you ever been fooled by someone you thought you loved?"

"I haven't…um, I haven't really any way to relate to that kind of situation. I've kept my life pretty simple. Career first. I didn't have time for relationships. At least, not any that lasted longer than a week." She slid a playful grin in place but evidently Evan wasn't in a joking mood for once. "Just ask my mother."

After a lingering stare, Evan pushed his glass away. He popped a half-melted ice cube into his mouth and crunched it. His Adam's apple bobbed up and down under the bronze skin of his throat.

Libby took another sip of her lemonade. She licked her lips and savored the lemon tang and hint of sugar. "So, just to be clear, you're not hurt that Angela is marrying someone else?"

Evan shook his head. "No. I had a bad case of self-pity after she broke off our engagement but looking back, I think I always had doubts. She loved my reputation and my money, but I'd probably never have explored that because...well, I'd made a commitment."

"That's noble."

Evan gave a careless shrug. "I felt gutted anyway. It hurt that someone who promised to love me no matter what didn't show up when I needed to be loved the most. I guess that's why I like good horses and kids. They're loyal."

"Molly told me when she and Bella first came back from our dad's ranch in New Mexico that Theo was getting bullied at school. Kids can be just as mean as adults. And horses buck."

"Some."

"Libby!" Molly interrupted their discussion. Her hair stood on end, and her blue peasant blouse had a large, white stain down the front.

"Hey, sis. You need a break, don't you?"

"Come here," Evan said in a cooing voice. He held out his arms for their red-faced niece. The baby squalled louder when the sun hit her eyes.

Molly handed the baby over and slumped into the chair between them. Libby poured her a glass of lemonade, added the lemon slice and mint sprig, and slid it in front of her with a sympathetic smile.

"She's teething," Evan said like he was the cowboy version of Doctor Spock.

"Again," Molly mumbled. She embraced the cold lemonade with both hands, closing her eyes as she sipped it like nectar. She cracked open a bleary eye. "You look good holding a baby, Evan."

Evan shot a look at Libby just as she'd raised her eyes to his face. Their eyes locked and he flushed a deeper bronze.

Libby's fair skin flared hot.

Molly looked between them, smirked, then closed her eyes again.

EVAN SNUGGLED baby Rose against his chest. She smelled like sour milk. He wrinkled his nose but pressed a kiss to her downy head. Holding her softened the painful fist that had taken hold inside his chest.

While Libby and Molly chatted, he soaked up the innocence of a new life. Rose had a blank slate. The world hadn't hurt her yet. Hadn't stolen a thing from her. She was being raised on a prosperous ranch in the cowboy culture where men protected their women and children. It was woven into their DNA by God Himself. Evan believed that with his whole heart. It was why he'd gone into the military. The call to protect and serve.

How was he going to do that now?

"As much as I'd like to sit here in the shade all day, sipping lemonade amongst you rich folks, I came to work," Libby said with a meaningful look at him. She was back to business. At least she was friendly about it.

Molly let out an exasperated sigh. "How is it that when nothing else works, Evan can always get Rose to sleep?"

Evan conjured a smile and winked at Libby. "Chicks dig me."

Molly scooped the baby into her arms and laughed. "Isn't that the truth? They always have." She turned to Libby. "Remember when everyone called him Superman in high school?"

A pretty blush stained Libby's cheeks. "Some people still do."

"If only your ego hadn't been even bigger than your biceps." Molly smirked at Evan.

His arms were as empty as his heart with baby Rose gone.

Molly jiggled the baby on her way inside, protecting her closed eyes from the glare of the sun with one hand.

He'd always feel empty without a family of his own. Might as well get used to it.

Libby traced the lip of her glass. "Well, you out-shadowed

every other guy in school sports, and I think there was more than one Evan McClure fan club among the freshman girls your senior year."

The corner of Evan's mouth lifted. "Not so much anymore, huh?" He wasn't really amused, and it wasn't really a question.

"Oh, I don't know. You're still turning heads, cowboy."

Was Libby genuine? Or was she shoveling empty flattery? She'd never been the type.

Evan snagged the tank top from the back of his chair, pulled it on, and ran a hand through his hair. "I suppose I could have come back with my face mangled instead of my body."

"Your face has only gotten better. As for the rest of you, have you checked out your upper body in a mirror lately? You're like a monster." She popped a raspberry into her mouth. "We'll start working your lower half more to balance things out when your hip isn't so sore."

Evan smiled. Libby had just admitted to checking him out.

"Your wranglers are lopsided." She grinned.

"Pardon?"

"Your left glute is underdeveloped. But we can work on that."

"Glad someone still notices how my butt looks like in jeans." He gave her his best wolfish grin. If ears really smoked, hers would be sending up signals. He'd better quit teasing her.

Of all the girls in their small high school, Libby had been the only one who never seemed to notice him. He'd thought her indifferent, but to be fair, she gave the same treatment to all the guys. Serious and studious, Libby Halverson released strong you-don't-stand-a-chance-vibes.

There had been a running bet about who could get a date with her during their last couple of years in Apple Valley High. Some of the guys had been overly confident in their abilities, and he'd been one of them. Whoever got a date with Libby would take home the cash pot they'd collected. It had only been pocket change to start with but by the end of their senior year it was up to a few hundred bucks. Nobody ever won it. *Where was that pot of cash now?*

"Evan?"

He jerked back to the present. "Sorry, guess I went wool gathering. What were you saying?"

"I asked if you're ready to get to work." Libby knit her brows. "Are you okay?"

"I'm fine." He zoomed in on her pale blue eyes. The gray around the irises was prominent today. "Libby, forget you're my physical therapist for a minute."

"Um…okay." Her voice was hesitant.

"When you look at me, what do you see? Total honesty."

She regarded him in silence. He couldn't read her. She dropped her eyes and studied her hands.

"Libby? Please," he said with equal parts pleading and teasing. He didn't want to be pathetic, after all.

Libby sighed and seemed to come to a decision after careful scrutiny of one of her fingernails. She met his eyes with a cool, direct gaze. She pressed her lips tight for a few seconds, as if reconsidering. "Evan, you've always been the biggest man in the room. The best looking, the strongest, the kindest, and the most charismatic. The past few years have taken a lot from you, but I still see that man. It's my job—my duty—to help you find him again."

He'd brightened inside at first. Until she said the word duty. He was just a job to her. What had he expected? He leaned forward, rested his arms on the table, and forced a confident smile. It was disingenuous of course, and she probably knew it.

What would Libby do if he kissed the impersonal right out of her?

He sat back. She'd probably smack him. And he'd deserve it. Libby was here to work. He should remember that. Besides, he wasn't who he used to be, was he?

Evan broke eye contact.

"Evan?" Her head was tilted to the side, brows furrowed. "Maybe we should postpone. You're off today."

"No."

Libby crossed her arms.

"I'm fine. Just wishing I could ride." It wasn't really a lie. "And I'm hungry. Haven't eaten yet."

Libby pushed her chair back and stood. Her tanned legs seemed to go on all day. She came near and put her hand on his shoulder. His bare skin reacted as if it had been hit by lightning. She smelled of lemon and sugar. He'd bet her mouth tasted like them, too.

"Why don't you get on your feet and let me watch you

walk a bit?" She moved her hand to the middle of his back, urging him with gentle pressure.

Tingles of heat licked his spine. He'd rather watch her walk.

He'd been sitting too long, and he swayed. Libby looped her arm around his waist, hugging his body snug against hers faster than he could blink. His pulse did a fast trot. Her throat was too near his mouth. His lips brushed the velvet skin as if by accident. It was like kissing a peach.

Libby helped him stand tall and then stood back like she'd been holding something hot. "A little dizzy, huh? Must be the heat." Her nervous giggle wasn't exactly professional.

Her reaction proved she wasn't as immune to him as she pretended. Good.

Evan reached out and brushed the inside of Libby's wrist, watching her face. "Thank you."

Libby's deep flush told him all he needed to know.

Chapter 6

ROWDY ROSEY

L ibby pressed her fingers to her throat where she'd swear Evan's mouth had brushed her skin. She shook her head at her imagination. Overactive hormones. She was bound for trouble unless she pushed away the attraction she'd never quite shaken. She hated to admit it, but that teenage girl with a wild crush still resided inside her after all these years.

She'd have to disappoint her.

All the way home, Evan's question wore a groove in her mind. What did she really think of him? No way could she admit the truth. That he was the most impressive example of masculinity she'd ever laid eyes on. Not a chance of her saying those words out loud. Nor would she say that his laugh made her toes tingle, that his boundless capacity for kindness had always touched her heart. She'd never say that his mere presence made the world go from single-tone gray to every sense on overload.

One leg or two, Evan was still a capable, handsome rancher who was going to dominate his corner of the world.

As soon as he remembered who he was.

She, on the other hand, had never forgotten. Evan was the one guy she'd measured every other guy against. It'd become her safety measure. She'd come to know herself well enough to understand she expected to be disappointed in love. Maybe Mom's midnight crying jags had made too deep an impression, but a belief had taken hold of her, and she couldn't shake it. A belief that if she let down her guard, she'd get a love 'em and leave 'em man like Mom had.

She'd never forget the winter they'd had to sell their horses to keep groceries in the house. Saying goodbye had brutalized her young heart, making their loss bigger to her than Dad leaving. The guy who didn't think his girls were worth staying for, or even providing for, had left them high and dry, and the taste of his abandonment and rejection stayed in her mouth.

She'd been a young teen with tender feelings about everything. Especially about her beautiful mother crying herself to sleep when she thought no one could hear her.

Her sisters hadn't let their temporary poverty stop them. Molly never batted one of her long eyelashes at the disparity between the bank accounts of the Halversons and the McClures. She and Cody had been crazy about each other since she was a freshman. Meanwhile, Josie tossed her gorgeous mane of dark hair and pursued a career as a western fashion model with confidence Libby had never been able to muster. They had a sense of themselves that she never had.

She couldn't believe she was worthy of a boy like Evan back then. The high school version of him had left every girl in town breathless. He was the larger-than-life guy in a letterman's jacket and snakeskin cowboy boots that other guys emulated, every girl swooned over, and every mother fawned over.

Libby blew a breath as she pulled into the farmhouse driveway. All of this introspection called for comfort measures. She changed into yoga pants and a ratty old T-shirt. Grandma Rose ignored her from the sofa, and Pumpkin melted into a heap near the stairs as Libby passed through to the porch and her favorite rocking chair.

Thirty-three and once again living in her childhood home. Now that she was searching for a way to live here for good, she could admit she'd been running for years. She imagined her grandfather's voice, his deep rumble, coming from the rocking chair next to her. You're letting life pass you by, Lisbeth.

"I know, Gramps," she said under her breath. He would have reminded her that her identity came from who she knew, not what she did. Jesus restored the dignity she had felt stolen by abandonment. He promised never to leave her. Grandpa rehearsed those words with a tender kiss to the top of her head more times than she could count. If only he could come back and do it one more time.

The sun was setting with hazy layers of purple overlapping pink hues. Libby glanced through the screen door. Grandma Rose's corgis, Bonnie and Clyde, snored at her feet. She perched on the sofa, engrossed in a Steven James thriller. His novels weren't Libby's taste, but Gram would get absorbed in them and not come up for air until she'd finished. Heaven help the fool who disturbed her.

A soft smile played on Libby's lips. There was an inspiring woman. "Rowdy Rosey" Cameron had married young, raised two daughters while working as hard as any wrangler on their ranch, and had managed their art gallery in town. Grandma Rose had ridden broncs on the weekends and even bucking bulls once or twice on dares or bets. Stories told it both ways. Grandpa Cameron used to brag on her. He'd never tried to stifle her wild ways. Josie was a lot like her. Libby, not so much. Steady was the word people often used to describe her.

Grandma had probably never been afraid of anything. She was fond of saying, "Trust the Lord, because He cares for His own. If you're one of His kids, you won't go without what you need." She'd said it before Grandpa died, and she'd said it afterward, too.

"I've lived my whole life running from something that wasn't even a threat," Libby confessed to Mom's tabby cat, curling around her ankles.

"Libby, honey, open the door," Grandma Rose called from the other side of the screen with a large bowl in each hand.

Libby pushed out of the rocker, opened the door, and took the bowls from her. "Yummy. Chocolate and cherry."

Gram trundled past her to sit in the other rocker. They savored their ice cream in silence for a while. A symphony from the pond creatures provided background music.

"Libby, what ever happened with that nice doctor you were seeing? Or that young financial advisor in Seattle? Ian Macsomebody."

"Ian MacTavish. He recently married a very sweet woman who runs a bed and breakfast on the west side of the mountains. Nice guy." She shrugged. "He just wasn't for me."

"And the doctor?" Grandma licked the back of her spoon like a child.

"He likes concrete, and I like grass."

Gram nodded. "When you finally choose your man, make sure he can hunt and fight. He'd better be able to light a fire and catch a fish." Her eyes sparked as she made a derisive sound. "A soft man in skinny jeans won't have much to offer you in a crisis."

Libby grinned and arched a brow. "Are you expecting a crisis?"

Gram turned her head sharply. "You never know. Anyhow, keep the western lifestyle alive, would you? The values of our community are dying out."

"Well, I came back home, didn't I?"

"I knew if you married a city boy, you'd regret it." Gram leaned in and gave her a sly look. "If you marry anyone but Evan McClure, you'll regret it." She started to dip her spoon in her bowl for another bite but pointed the spoon at Libby instead. "Don't bother denying it." She furrowed her brows. "You never fooled your grandpa, either. He liked Evan and approved of the match."

"What match?" Libby scoffed. "Evan and I were never a

match and honestly, sometimes I think you need your filter changed. You say the most shocking things."

"What happened that time he asked you on a date in high school?"

"Evan?" Libby frowned. "That was a bet. Cody told Molly all about the wager going on between Evan and his friends and she told me."

"Oh, yes. The bet."

"You knew?"

"This is a small town, remember. There isn't much I don't know and quite a bit I wish I didn't."

Libby bit into a chunk of tart cherry. "You know, a few months after that incident I was gathering up the courage to ask Evan to the next dance. I'd just gotten my plan all worked out…"

"And?" Gram demanded with her spoon halted mid-way to her mouth.

"Angela asked him first. The rest, as they say, is history."

Grandma Rose crossed her bunny slippers at the ankles. "I'm glad I had the gumption to tell your grandfather how I felt about him. We built a good life together. He'd be proud of all his girls."

A little achy spot for her wonderful grandfather had mellowed but never quite left her heart. "I miss him."

"So do I. He was my best friend." Gram leaned forward. "But you know, I might have missed out on him. He was a Cameron after all, and Camerons were money back then. My family had moved to the valley as Scandinavian immigrants.

They worked as migrant fruit pickers." Gram scratched her nose. "My parents eventually settled and bought a small place outside of the town proper. I think everyone was shocked when I married into the Cameron family."

"How did you meet?" She knew the story well but never tired of hearing it.

"It was a beautiful summer morning. The light was weak, but sufficient. Fog was crawling up from the lake and just prowling around the trees, the way a cat does. You know that slow, sinuous movement, wrapping itself around your legs." She toed the side of the purring tabby. "I'd come to paint the sunrise and so had Hamish. We were both aspiring artists. I wasn't very good, but Hamish was gifted. He humored me and let me paint with him."

"You were his biggest fan." Libby relished the idea of her grandparents as young, unlined—and as yet untouched by sorrow. She'd often stared at a picture hanging on the living room wall of her grandfather as a young man. He'd been strong and kissed by the sun then. Near the end of his life, sallow and skeletal, he didn't resemble that photo at all except for his eyes.

"Hamish was mine. He was the handsomest, funniest man I'd ever met. It didn't hurt one bit that he was kind and rich. I let his family's status in the valley keep us apart the first year. But soon enough the thought of losing him to another girl got me riled enough to just get over the money."

They were silent for a few breaths. It was Libby's turn. She knew her part. "Where did you two share your first kiss?"

"Underneath an old apple tree—the same one where we'd bumped into one another with our easels and paint pots. That tree still stands on the old homestead that belongs to you now."

They went on until their bowls were empty. Telling. Listening. Asking. The story of her great romance was interactive when Grandma Rose told it. She expected participation.

"You're going to stay on in Apple Valley?" Gram faced her.

Libby toed the cat's fur. "I've decided to find a way."

"Good."

Libby's cell phone played Molly's ringtone from inside the house. "Excuse me, Gram." She took their empty bowls with her. For some reason the little gold hairs on her arms were standing up. She picked up her phone. Molly's photo appeared on the screen and Libby swiped to answer.

"Hi, what's up?"

"Lib, Evan's spending the night in the hospital. You won't need to come to work in the morning. Maybe not for a few days depending on what the doctor says."

Libby's stomach dropped. "What happened?"

"The dummy got on a two-year old colt and didn't just get dumped—he got wrecked." Molly's tone was weary.

"A colt? Evan isn't even cleared to ride. There must be a mistake."

"No mistake, sis. You know how stubborn cowboys are and the McClures in particular. This might have cost him the implant."

"Are you home?"

"Yes, I'm going to get the kids ready for bed. Cody said I should let you know what happened. I'll call again if I hear anything new."

"I'm going to see for myself in the morning. You have enough on your plate, so don't try to take on the job of third-party communication."

"Okay. Night."

"Good night."

Libby put her palm over her hollow stomach. Why were men so determined to self-destruct?

EVAN'S STUMP ached like a rotten tooth, but he'd refused pain meds. He gritted his teeth at a sharp stab of pain in his right shoulder. It traveled down his arm, making his hand go numb. His left wrist didn't feel so hot either.

He shouldn't have allowed himself to be goaded into riding a green colt. Libby and Molly were right about his ego. It'd shrunk considerably since he got flung out of his saddle like a ragdoll in front of a dozen other cowboys. He'd let a local hotshot bareback rider hassle him, and he was paying the price flat on his back in a hospital bed.

Again.

He was an idiot.

The curtains in his hospital room were gathered tight to keep out the late morning sun. Too bad they couldn't shut out the reel looping in his head. He was destined to spend time in the dirt. The Three M wranglers had tried to stop him from taking the bet that Dennis, a day worker from Wyoming, had thrown down. But when the guy sneered and pointed to Evan's prosthetic, he couldn't see his way clear to backing down. The loud-mouthed drifter spat in the dirt and bet that Evan couldn't stay on that rank colt for eight seconds. The horse had injured two interns the week before. That's why he was in a holding pen, slated to go to the sale barn.

Like a mindless trout, Evan had swallowed the worm.

As soon as he could move without passing out, he'd find that Dennis guy and pay him the twenty bucks he owed him.

Twenty bucks. He'd risked his life for a twenty-dollar bill. Even worse, risked his chance to *ever* ride again.

The nagging beep of machines rankled him. The flirtatious nurse who popped in and out of his room at inopportune moments—like when he'd had to use the urinal—rankled him. Her squeaky voice and too-bright smile rankled him. In fact, there wasn't a single thing that didn't tick him off about being helpless as a baby again.

When he closed his eyes, he saw himself as a little old man, hunched over a desk in the ranch office, cutting paychecks for cowboys doing work he was born to do.

He'd kick himself, but he only had one leg. And besides, as a parting shot when he was down, the colt kicked him right in the back pocket. He had a perfect hoof print on his butt, or so he was told. The nurse had offered to hold a mirror to his backside for him. He'd declined and been none too polite about it.

Evan tried to take pressure off his bruised side, but there

wasn't any place that didn't hurt. He clenched his jaw, his eyes, and his fists.

"Mr. McClure!" The nurse's exuberant voice jarred his aching bones.

He cracked one eye just enough to peek through. Maybe she'd go away if he ignored her.

"Don't try to pretend you're asleep. I brought your lunch." She giggled and lifted a tray like she was delivering a gourmet treat. The hot smell of something savory mixed with the hospital's chemical odors and made him want to bring up the lump of tile grout from breakfast that she'd called oatmeal.

Boots clomped just outside Evan's hospital room. "We've come to save you, brother." Cody's voice sounded like fiddle music to Evan's ears.

Theo's head appeared around the corner, cautious as a turtle poking out of its shell.

Evan struggled to sit up. The nurse hustled to set the tray down and fluff his pillows. She fussed with his I.V. and sheets. "I just need to get a set of vitals before you eat." Before Evan could refuse, she pushed a thermometer under his tongue.

"Ow!"

"Shhhh." She glanced at her watch.

Cody snickered.

Waggling his eyebrows like caterpillars, Evan waved Theo inside.

Cody jerked his head to one side and swung a Major's Burgers bag out from behind his back, then hid it when the nurse turned to smile at them.

"Are you family? You look a lot alike."

"Normally, I wouldn't claim him, but yeah, we're brothers." Cody leaned toward her to offer a handshake and squinted at her name badge. "Pleased to meet you, Daphne. I'm Cody McClure." He kept the burger bag out of sight.

A coy smile formed on Daphne's lips, and she batted her lashes. "Nice to meet you, Cody."

"This is my son, Theodore. Theo, come say howdy."

Theo stepped forward and dipped his head, lips sealed.

"I take it you're Evan's nurse today." Cody patted Theo's head in a reassuring manner.

"I'm the nurse's assistant. Barbara is the nurse in charge." Daphne bared coffee-stained teeth. "She's the tall one with white streaks in her hair."

"Gotcha," Cody said. "We can help Evan with his lunch. I'm sure you have more important things to do."

She made a sound of protest, but Cody held up his hand. "No bother."

Daphne scribbled down Evan's temperature, blood pressure, and a few more numbers from the monitor. She checked the level of his fluid bag and his I.V. site again, then motioned for him to roll to the side as she lifted the sheet away from his lower half.

Evan glared and snatched the sheet back.

"I'm supposed to document the swelling and bruising."

"Later," Evan growled.

"Simmer down, cowboy." She was clearly miffed. "Use the call button if you need anything."

"Will do," Cody said in a cheery voice. Knowing him, he was trying to make up for Evan's surly behavior.

Evan eyed the tray of hospital food with disdain. The meals were notoriously bad, and he'd had his share of them in the past. "I'm glad to see you two. I thought she was going to smile me to death."

Cody laughed. "Come on. It could have been worse. Remember that grumpy old nurse you had a couple of years ago? She had a long, gray braid…what was her name?"

"Elsa?" Theo took a guess.

Grinning, Cody tousled his hair. "Maybe you're right, bud." He turned to Evan. "Hungry?"

Evan shook his pounding head. "Not really."

"Well, you'd better try to eat this double bacon cheese-burger while it's hot and before Daphne comes back to make sure you're eating—" He lifted the lid on the plate in the center of the hospital meal tray. "Umm…well, whatever that is." He wrinkled his nose, set the tray aside, and dropped the burger bag in its place. "Brought curly fries, too.

Theo slinked over to the hospital bed with concern in his little almond-shaped eyes. "And a strawberry shake, your favorite." He handed the clear plastic cup to Evan.

Cody stepped forward and jabbed a straw through the hole in the lid. "Eat up."

Clenching his jaw, Evan lifted his weight to pull himself higher in the bed. A jolt of pain ran down his neck, and another fired through his shoulder. His lower back spasmed, and his implant site…well, that area of his body was being stomped by a mad bull. He was sure of it just now. He lifted the crisp hospital sheet. The scents of dried blood and iodine wafted from underneath. "Why is it all bandaged?"

"Your prosthetic landed at an angle. If it had been flesh and bone it'd be broken. As it is, you may need surgery to straighten or replace the implant. But if the connection with the bone has been damaged...well, we can cross that bridge if we come to it. The MRI they took this morning will tell us what we need to know. Your specialist from Seattle is on his way to read it and give his opinion."

Evan set the shake aside with a trembling hand. The aroma of bacon, beef, and fries would normally rouse his interest no matter what was going on, but just now they nauseated him. He gave Theo a wobbly smile. "You know Seattle traffic. This might take all day." His voice was hoarse, and Theo noticed. Evan inhaled courage and smiled for his nephew. "Come up here and help me eat, kiddo."

"You mean you need me to feed you?" Theo asked. His eyes rounded as if to say, *"It's worse than I thought."*

"No. I'm just not that hungry, and there's no reason to let a Major's double bacon cheeseburger go to waste."

"We already ate," Theo admitted.

"I see. And where's your sister? Did Bella stay home to watch those naughty, trouble-making poodles?" He teased, wanting to ease the worry on Theo's face.

Theo's mouth lifted but it was a half-hearted effort. "They aren't naughty, Uncle Evan. They only chase chickens is all."

"Did I hear there's a Major's cheeseburger going to waste

in here?" Libby stood in the doorway, arms crossed, and one cowboy boot in the hall as if she weren't sure she was coming in all the way.

Was she here to tell him off for the risk he'd taken? Point out the damage he'd done to himself?

Cody leaned down and said something in a low tone to Theo that Evan didn't catch. Theo nodded. His eyes darted from Libby to Evan and back again.

"It's time to see if Mom needs help with baby Rose. We'll see you later, Uncle Evan." Theo closed the gap to Evan's bedside and patted his forearm before backing away again. "Excuse me," he said to Libby as he passed her in the doorway.

The hospital held upsetting memories for Theo. He'd been a fragile infant, needing surgery and care. It was also the place he'd been parted from his biological mother when she'd abandoned him without ever even holding him.

"See you later, Theo." Libby knelt to hug him.

Warmth spread in Evan's chest. She'd seen Theo's discomfort. That was one more thing he liked about Libby—she noticed people. The way she wore cowboy boots with a short skirt, showing off long, tan legs didn't hurt either.

"Libby, you might as well tuck into those curly fries before they go limp and cold," Cody advised. He shot a meaningful look at Evan. "Brother." He nodded and trailed Theo out of the room.

"I'm starving." Libby snatched the warm, oil-splotched bag and plopped into the chair facing the foot of Evan's hospital bed. She crossed her cowboy boots at the ankles on the end of the bed and rummaged inside the bag. She bit off the end of a fry and closed her eyes, moaning in delight. Her eyes opened and locked on Evan as she ate the other half. Then she pulled out the burger and held it in the air. Major's burgers were famous for their size and meaty, salty goodness. "You know I can't eat this whole thing." She took a bite and rolled her eyes. "But I might just try."

Evan's stomach growled.

Libby covered her full mouth and snorted. She finished chewing, stood up, and offered the burger to Evan. "I figured that would work."

"We can share." Evan's mouth tipped up on one side even though he'd tried his best not to smile at her. He took the burger and bit into it. Delicious.

Libby parted the curtains. "It's a gorgeous day."

The sun shone through the window and spun strands of Libby's hair into gold. A cinnamon sprinkle of freckles across her nose and cheeks made him want to count them.

With his lips.

"I really am hungry." Libby snatched another fry and bit into it. "They salt these perfectly, don't they?"

Evan was about to take another bite when he noticed a sprinkle of salt on Libby's bottom lip that caused his tongue to stick to the roof of his mouth. He reached for the strawberry shake instead. After a long pull on the straw, he scooted up, stifling a groan of pain as he did.

Libby watched him closely, then bent close enough for their noses to touch. "I want another bite."

Evan's pulse skittered like a scared calf. For sure now, any minute, the monitor connected to his heart was going to sound an alarm and tell on him.

Libby took a slow, deliberate bite of the cheeseburger with her eyes glued to his. She straightened, sat in the chair next to his bed, and stared him down. "I know what you're thinking, Evan, and it's not true."

Surely, Libby did *not* know what he was thinking right now, or else she'd have already smacked him.

Chapter 7

WAR STORIES

"What is it you think I'm thinking?" Evan's voice was strained. Blotches of color rose from his neck into his cheeks.

Libby wiped her mouth. Her half of the bacon cheeseburger had hit the spot. So she'd used the opportunity of sharing Evan's dinner to flirt with him? So what? She'd meant to provoke him. He didn't need pity right now. He needed to be reminded he was a man.

She refused to let another injury steer them off course from his goals. She could hide the fact that she'd like to throttle him right about now.

She took her time brushing crumbs from the short cotton skirt she'd chosen on purpose, then looked up and squared off with him. "You think that wreck yesterday derailed your recovery."

"Maybe it did." He wasn't petulant, but he wasn't far from

it. "My Dad's freeze branding the year-old calves. I should be helping."

"Yes. You should."

Evidently, he wasn't expecting her to say that because his head snapped up.

The time for sympathy and excuses was over. It was time for some tough love.

"The specialist is on his way, huh?" Libby stood and walked to the window. Her cotton skirt floated around her legs, just above her knees. She turned from the parking lot view to find Evan wiping perspiration from his forehead. She hid a smile. She'd made him sweat. Good. "I've met him on a few occasions in patient care meetings." She rearranged her skirt for Evan's benefit.

"I've met him once or twice." He arched a brow and squirmed.

"Our goals don't change, Evan. No matter what he says today."

He closed his eyes and turned his face to the wall. "I'm going to wind up in a wheelchair again. Sitting in an office all day."

"Only if you choose that."

Evan turned snapping eyes on her.

Yep, he was provoked.

"Am I supposed to just will my old self back?"

"The Evan I grew up with was resilient. Strong. Determined."

His face sagged. "That was a long time ago."

Libby sat on the edge of his bed, tugging her skirt down for modesty. She did have boundaries. "There's something special about you. Everyone sees that *but* you. Why is that?"

Evan looked away. "It's your job to feed me lines like that."

"Oh please. When have you known me to be fake?"

"The only girl who wouldn't date me is telling me how great I am all of a sudden." The hint of a smile lifted his lips. The old Evan was still there somewhere. She was catching a glimpse now.

Her stomach fluttered at the shape his mouth was taking. If he weren't at a disadvantage both physically and emotionally, she might dare to plant a kiss on that mouth. Instead, she leaned back. "The only time you asked me on a date, you did it because of a bet. I heard about you and the other jocks wagering on me."

"We did have a bet going. For two years." He chuckled. "But the thing is, you never looked at me like the other girls did. In fact, you barely noticed me at all."

"You thought I didn't notice you, and that was a blow to your ego, huh?"

He shrugged one shoulder. A tightening of his features showed the gesture caused pain. "I wasn't used to being ignored. I even dated a few college girls. Why do you think the other guys thought I was so cool?" Evan grinned. His muscles loosened visibly as they flirted.

Libby rolled her eyes. "The other guys admired you for lots

of reasons besides your ability to lure silly girls into dark corners."

"Hey now." Evan protested but it was halfhearted.

"The truth was, I made sure you didn't see me turn red as a cherry every time you passed by." Libby twisted a corner of the napkin she'd used to wipe her mouth.

"You did not." He angled his chin up to challenge her.

The look in his eyes was an arrow right to the center of her heart. But it was liberating to tell him the truth. She'd been just as crazy about him as all the other girls. She'd have been boiled alive before telling him, but right now he needed to hear it.

She took a breath for courage. "I even tried to ask you out once."

"You never did."

"I did," she argued. "Angela asked you to the Tolo dance about five minutes before I got to the football field for the same reason. Believe me, I heard all about it. So did everyone else. I'm surprised it wasn't featured on the local news that evening. Your life was the most interesting thing happening in Apple Valley."

"Libby, what would have happened if you'd said yes to me when I asked you out? Or if you'd gotten to the field before Angela?"

She shrugged a how-should-I-know? "Grandpa Cameron used to tell us that God works on His own timeline, and we should be grateful He does. We'd just mess things up if it were left to us."

"Sometimes I don't like the way God operates." Evan's eyes traveled down to his newly injured amputation site under the stark, white sheet.

"Yeah. Me neither. But He doesn't promise us that we won't experience pain. Or trouble. Just the opposite. He promises that He will be with us even if we bring trouble on ourselves. If someone else piles trouble on us, He's our defender."

Evan was silent and brooding for a long moment before he said, "When I was dying in the sand with my leg blown off, deaf from the blast, I felt Him. The shock, the fear, all of it lifted when He came. Everything returned later, but for that time…He was there with me."

An image of Evan's beautifully formed body lying in a pool of blood with charcoal-stained blast marks on his skin made her shudder. To think of Evan as vulnerable to an enemy, bleeding out where his leg had been severed, sickened her. Libby used to think of him as invincible. The scene in her imagination was unwanted. She'd seen numerous photos of accidents and attacks in her ongoing education classes.

Evan was watching her. Gauging her reaction?

"Another man—a man who'd lost both his legs in a car accident a few years ago, had a similar experience. I've never forgotten the way he told the story and always wondered…if I were to find myself in a terrible circumstance, would God really come to comfort me?"

Evan nodded with his lips pressed tight, tears filling his

eyes. "Yes. He's that kind of God. But I hope you'll never need Him like that."

Libby gave his hand a squeeze and swallowed hard.

Evan cleared the emotion from his throat. "I was scared when I woke. When I learned Dave didn't make it, guilt ate me up. I wondered why Dave died but God allowed me to live. Dave was the better man. I resented this body that didn't feel like mine anymore. I was jealous of Dave. I had to live the rest of my life maimed."

Evan met her eyes. "I hated that Dave was dead. I grieved him. But the loss I had to live with—my leg, my future wife, my livelihood—was too much to ask." Evan sighed and fixed a stare on the wall. "Dave and I used to make plans. We were going to come home, meet up for summer BBQs, and laugh about all the stupid stuff we did in our Army days. I was supposed to marry Angela and raise a bunch of kids. I dreamed of building my own herd of cattle and competing in the local rodeos. I just wanted to serve my country and then resume my life." His voice grew wistful. "A small, happy life."

"But things didn't go the way you planned, and now you must learn new ways to live." It wasn't lost on her that Evan had trusted her enough to unload his emotional baggage at her feet.

"Angela was a rejection. One more gut punch in a series of them. But the worst was that I lost who I used to be. Or, who I thought I was."

"You may have one less leg, but you're more man than ever. You left a boy behind in that sand. A popular boy who charmed this whole town with winning looks and touchdowns. You're still Superman, Evan. Who else would even want to run a big ranch and raise cattle with a prosthetic leg?" Libby dared Evan to contradict her. He was no Luke Conner, she was sure of that now, but Evan hadn't yet caught that glimpse of his inner strength. Strength of character he'd need to propel him forward to meet his goals.

Evan gave her a sad smile. "We'll see what the specialist says. Will you stay and hear the MRI results with me?"

"If you want me to be here. But no matter what he says, we're going to start over. I've been researching various ways to strengthen and lengthen the muscles you need to ride. Massage therapy will help, too. I brought my iPad to show you some videos of other athletes who have had Osseointegration. They're really inspiring."

Evan closed his eyes.

He's afraid to hope. Libby settled her hand on his chest, enjoying the rise and fall for a minute before she said, "I can't *make* you be successful, but I can *help* you be successful. Your only ceiling—truly—is your mind."

His lips pulled up in a grin. "Massage therapy, huh?" He peeked at her out of one twinkling eye.

Libby pulled his earlobe.

"Ouch!" He furrowed his brows. "You're just as mean as ever, aren't you?"

"Yes. And I want you to know, I'm not giving up. If I have to kick your Wrangler-wrapped butt into the workout room every single day, I'll do it."

"I think my family would help you." He opened both eyes and stared at the ceiling. "Getting thrown on my can from that colt is going to make this so much harder."

"Yes, it is." There was no point in lying to him.

"But you're going to stick with me?"

"I'm here, aren't I?"

Evan relaxed into the pillow. His mouth lifted in a heart-melting smile, and she whispered a pleading prayer to heaven for a good report. He was clinging to hope by a fragile thread, and she had no idea what the specialist might say.

LIBBY'S FINGERS dug into Evan's arm as they waited for the surgeon to explain the MRI results. Dr. Walden frowned at a tablet in his hands. It was nice to have Libby stick around for support, but did she have to give him new injuries on top of the bruises and lacerations he already had?

The doctor's balding head reflected the yellow lights above him. Little tufts of hair around his ears gave the impression that the hair was coming from inside his ears. The guy was overdue for a visit to his barber.

Evan pried Libby's fingers loose with a gentle hand and reassuring smile. She was breathing a prayer, her lips barely moving. He glanced between Libby and the doctor. Just when he thought he might explode, the doctor finally looked up.

"Mr. McClure, the MRI indicates severe inflammation, but the bone growth has— surprisingly, in my opinion—not been disturbed." His expression was severe. "However, things could have gone terribly wrong. It's my duty to warn you that another incident like that may very well damage the bone growth and make another implant impossible."

"So, everything is fine then." Evan unclenched his hands. The hours he'd spent waiting for news had twisted his guts in knots.

"As I said, you might have caused—"

"Doctor, sorry to disturb you, but you have an emergency call." A tall woman wearing blue scrubs and a stethoscope around her neck leaned her arms on either side of the door. She vanished after Dr. Walden gave her a clipped nod.

Evan thanked the doctor's back as he scurried away. He turned to high-five Libby, but she collapsed in a chair with her bottom lip between her teeth.

Evan propped himself up. "What are you so worked up about? An hour ago, you were talking about having faith and thinking positive and—"

"Shut up, Evan," she said very quietly and closed her eyes.

A scuffling in the hall drew his attention to the doorway. Cody and Dad hustled in and looked around the room. "Hey, did we miss the doctor or are you still waiting?"

"He just left and it's all good," Evan said nonchalantly. Inside, he wanted to bust into a million pieces. He'd been tormented about what the doctor might say. He could not under any circumstance be bound to a wheelchair or a bed again.

He'd never risk another injury.

But was that even living? He wanted to be the man he used to be. The one Libby kept telling him he still was.

THE NEXT DAY, after the doctor released him with a promise of restricted activity, Evan hauled himself back in the workout room. It tore at him to use the wheelchair to get around the ranch again. He'd get back out of it as soon as he could.

Grandpa Smokey sat on a chair, sipping lemonade, and counting reps for him. "That's twenty now, time for a rest."

Evan melted back on the bench to catch his breath, one arm pinning the other over his chest. His ribs ached, and his implant site was on fire, but he was going to get every exercise crossed off his list before he quit. His arm was supposed to be in a sling for a few weeks but there was no way to balance his body with one arm out of service, nor could he wheel his chair with one arm.

Libby was scheduled to attend a conference, so Grandpa had volunteered to supervise Evan's therapy. When Libby tried to cancel her plans, Evan insisted she go ahead. He didn't want her to think he couldn't manage without her. He sure did miss her though. They'd been together for weeks on end. She'd become his head cheerleader. Even if she was a cheerleader wielding a cattle prod. He recalled her scowl as she lectured him before leaving for the trip over the mountains.

Grandpa Smokey eyed him, seemed to consider something, then laughed a huff of air. "She'll be back soon enough."

Evan gave him a stink eye.

"It's time you married." Grandpa's rough voice was tinged with humor.

"A broken down, one-legged cowboy is not exactly every woman's fantasy."

Grandpa made a disapproving noise. "A wealthy rancher with miles and miles of potential is, though. Especially Apple Valley's own darling, as you've always been." He pointed a gnarled finger in Evan's direction. "Now that you have a new-fangled prosthetic leg with a computer inside it, you'll be bionic, not just super."

Evan lifted a brow.

"You're cowboy-tough, and part owner of fruitful land. Land that'll only make its owners richer. You're a man this town loves to love. Why not become a man who inspires other veterans—especially amputees—by setting an example of get-after-it and get 'er done?" Grandpa Smokey took a pocketknife from a case on his belt and began to pare his nails. He'd always trimmed them that way. It used to drive Grandma McClure nuts.

Evan pulled himself up with his abs and groaned at the toll on his rib cage.

"What if you pave the way for others to overcome their limitations? There's purpose in everything, thanks to God. He's a giver. When did you forget that?"

"You sound like Libby."

"She's one smart lady. The fact that she's crazy about you proves it."

"Sometimes I flatter myself that she's interested. But then I'm reminded that her reputation is riding on how successful I am with the Osseointegration."

"Ha." Grandpa waved his hand to dismiss Evan's words. "The girl is quick-witted and good at what she does. Libby doesn't need you. She *wants* you. She's had other job opportunities, but she's refused them."

A tingle of apprehension tripped down Evan's spine. "How do you know that?"

"Rosey told me. She also said she signed over the old Cameron homestead to Libby."

Evan made a noncommittal noise, sat upright, and swiveled on the bench. "Doesn't Lefty Hanson live there?"

"That's a pickle, but I told Rosey we'd figure something out. Lefty needs a job and a place to stay."

"He's too old to start over," Evan protested. "He's a Vietnam vet. You can't just evict him."

"No, but Rose has been paying the electric bill, and she won't expect Libby to continue that. Besides, Libby will want to move in, I'd expect."

"Doubtful. The old place has fallen into ruin the last few years."

"Nothin' a bit of elbow grease can't fix." Grandpa slipped the handful of nail parings into his pocket and sheathed his knife. "You ought to be glad she's settling down. She might have taken a job in Colorado if Rosey hadn't stepped in."

His heart would crumble like dry cornbread if Libby left. "She's a career-minded woman. I doubt very much she'd aspire to be a combat-wounded rancher's wife. That comes with all kinds of baggage. As we've all experienced, I'm a full-time job." Evan drank the dregs from his water bottle and tossed it across the room into the garbage can.

Grandpa Smokey took a thoughtful sip of his lemonade. Evan wouldn't mind a glass of cold lemonade.

As if reading his mind, Grandpa got up on creaky legs and poured him one.

"Thanks." Evan drained the glass and gave it back.

"Another?"

"No, thanks." He started his stretching routine. He focused on the muscles that weren't injured. They were few. "Did you ever regret serving?"

"Of course. Vietnam was a terrible place." His voice was raspy. "A terrible time. I couldn't shake some of the things I'd seen, smelled, or heard."

"I can relate."

"I served with a few men who had to do things they couldn't live with. Once they returned stateside those things ate their guts."

Evan kept his lips tight. He hadn't done things to haunt him later, but many had.

"So many never made it home." Grandpa Smokey pulled at the corners of his mustache. "Vietnam scarred me. But because God spared me, I married the girl of my dreams, and she gave me some fine sons." He clapped a hand on Evan's shoulder. "I inherited this ranch from my father and divided it among my sons, as you know. I trusted God to make a way for me." He fixed a penetrating eye on Evan. "He did. You boys and all your cousins are my legacy. Life is precious and costly, but it's worth living."

"I'm still angry Dave didn't come home. Angry my leg didn't either."

Grandpa Smokey grunted. "I came home angry, too. It didn't help that people called us names and spit on us. Some made us feel like we were monsters."

"You ever have nightmares?"

Grandpa Smokey nodded. "We were just kids. Draft numbers, to the government." He rubbed his throat.

He had never mentioned the war before, nor how he felt about it.

"Sometimes at night in the jungle, I'd hear boys crying. That's all we mostly were, you know. Just boys. We missed our mamas and our friends and our girls." He stood and straightened the buttons on his shirt. When he spoke again his voice was firm. "What if you allowed the hardship to toughen you? Make you a stronger man? You have resources. Use them. Build a bridge for other veterans." Grandpa walked toward the door. He had a permanent limp from an old cow punching injury, but it never cut into his dignity.

Men respected Smokey McClure. For as long as Evan could remember, he'd always wanted to grow up to be just like his grandpa.

Grandpa Smokey's words prodded places Evan kept stuffed down. Questions he'd shelved for too long.

What was required of him?

He spread his fingers wide and stared at his hands. Ranching was in his blood. He was born to it. But he'd had a life-altering experience. He needed something positive to come of it for it to make sense.

Grandpa Smokey's suggestion stirred something inside his soul that had gone dormant. Every generation had its tragedies.

This was his.

With difficulty, he kneeled, closed his eyes, and promised God that from now on, he would dominate his limitations and use his prosthetic leg to kick down doors.

No more self-pity.

Chapter 8

HOW SUPERMAN WAS BORN

Libby breathed in the fresh scents of apples and just-mown rows of grass between the trees of the McClure's orchard. A soft breeze played with her hair and her mount's forelock as she and Evan rode horseback through acres of Golden Delicious apples. The trees dripped in small, green orbs. They wouldn't be ripe for another two months but that didn't stop the stocky buckskin gelding she rode from trying to snatch one when they brushed a limb hanging heavy with low-hanging fruit. Honeybees buzzed with happy tunes around the desert wildflowers. At least they sounded happy to her. Maybe she was influenced by her own heart. A long, lazy trail ride was the cure she'd needed. Too bad she hadn't picked a more level-headed horse.

Her old insecurities were bubbling to the surface now that she was back home. Josie had accused her of being wishy-washy on the phone yesterday. "Everyone knows how you feel about Evan. Quit making excuses and just go for it."

Go for it? Josie always made everything sound like a simple matter. Wishy-washy? That part was true.

It had been three weeks since Evan had been dumped from the back of an ornery colt. It must have knocked some sense into him because he had more focus than ever. Therapy was going well. Here they were, on horseback. Wasn't that what Alex McClure paid her to do? Get his eldest son back to work on the ranch?

But what would happen when Evan no longer needed therapy? She'd helped one or two of the wranglers who worked for the McClures when they'd pulled a muscle or twisted an ankle, but too soon her services would no longer be required at the Three M.

She'd have to figure out what to do about the squatter on her land. What would she do with the property once he was gone? She had to have money to develop the old home into something that would keep her here.

A Kestrel called to its mate from a fence post, startling her borrowed horse. When Toby picked his ears up once more Libby patted his neck and praised him. A rabbit bolted from a nearby clump of sagebrush and the buckskin jumped in the air with all four feet. Libby settled him and began to wish she'd chosen the dappled gray gelding that she'd been offered first. He'd had a lazy look to him, so she'd chosen Toby instead.

Evan kept an eye on her but kept his mouth shut about the horse and how she handled him. He pointed to a badger's den next to the fence on the other side of the tree row. "I saw prints earlier. Was wondering if we might come across his hole."

"Better than a rattlesnake den I suppose." Libby adjusted her cap to shield her face from the July sun. The last thing she needed was more freckles.

Evan eyed her. "Let's move to the shaded side of the trail."

She'd agreed to let Evan ride if she accompanied him. Being astride seemed to make him more hopeful about reaching his goals. As for dancing the two-step, that didn't seem likely by August. Putting his weight on the implant site for too long caused more inflammation and pain.

A coyote ran across the trail ahead of them. It vanished into the trees just as a Gopher Snake slithered over the grass in front of Toby's hooves. Libby focused on tuning into her unfamiliar mount as he danced in agitation. She had to be vigilant with this horse. She couldn't say she hadn't been warned.

The path narrowed so Evan moved ahead on his bay Quarter Horse. He'd had a lighter-boned chestnut he rode to calf-roping events in high school, but that horse was retirement age. Emmet was seasoned and had been deemed a safe bet for their trail rides.

Libby let her thighs relax against Toby's sides as she enjoyed an inspiring view of Evan's broad back. His muscles stretched a navy-blue T-shirt and curls escaped to graze his collar. In worn Wranglers and a light gray Stetson, he was downright swoon-worthy.

"Are you disappointed you missed out on the rodeo?"

Libby called to the blue T-shirt her eyes had been riveted on for the past few minutes.

"Sure." Evan glanced over his shoulder but faced forward again when a quail family flushed out of the tall grass to their right.

Libby released a breath when Emmet merely flicked an ear and walked on. "There's always next year if you team rope in the spring."

"How is it that a beautiful, smart woman like you has managed to stay unattached this long?" Evan reined Emmet over so she could come alongside with Toby. He leaned over the pommel to blow a butterfly away from Emmet's ear. The bay merely shook his head. Unlike Toby, who stamped his foot impatiently every time they stopped.

She noted Evan's lips were pressed thin and white around the edges. He smiled and pretended he was enjoying himself. Maybe he was, but he was also in discomfort. Libby gave Toby a squeeze to move ahead when he started pawing the ground. "You and I are not going on a second date, horse." She averted her eyes. Evan had asked her a question she had no intention of answering.

"He needs more saddle time," Evan said. He rode along-side her at a leisurely pace.

For the next ride, she'd be sure to ask for a different mount. It didn't help that an obstinate, dry wind kicked up, teasing the buckskin's mane. He was having a good time pretending to get spooked by it. Libby tucked a wisp of her own hair back into her ponytail and tightened it at her nape.

The high desert weather was changeable and dark clouds moved over them.

"You didn't answer me." Evan was going to pursue his line of questioning.

Libby shifted her gaze sideways. He was laughing at her. Well, he'd bared his soul to her back in the hospital. Maybe she should give a little, too. "You asked for it."

"Give me all you got." His eyes challenged her.

She glanced up as the gloomy clouds passed and the sun broke through. "After my dad left us, we had a tough year. The novelty of poverty wore off real quick. After a talk with the school counselor one day, I decided to make sure I was never at the mercy of fate and a fickle man again. Instead, I'd focus on my education. I made plans to pursue a career so I could take care of myself. Back then I thought Mom's biggest mistake was choosing to be a homemaker because it made her vulnerable."

"But now?"

"Now I'm confident that her choice of husband was the problem."

"Ouch. You're not close with your dad?"

"Let's just say it took me *years* to forgive him, and I still don't like him."

Evan glanced at her. "Sounds like you're still workin' on that. Your experience left you with a negative view of men?"

Libby stiffened in her saddle, and Evan raised a hasty hand. "I didn't mean that the way it sounded."

"How did you mean it?" She gave him a cold look.

Evan grimaced.

Maybe it was time for a break. "Why don't we sit and watch that hawk?" Libby pointed to a red-tailed hawk near a clump of sagebrush, devouring the remnants of some hapless creature.

She swung off Toby's back, then held Emmet's reins while Evan dismounted. Evan limped to a large rock and sat with his prosthetic elevated on a smaller rock.

After tying the horses, Libby perched on a rock opposite him. The hawk eyed them but went on eating.

Staring up at the sky, Evan's exposed throat bobbed in a swallow. He removed his sunglasses and hat. A wrinkle cut across the expanse of his forehead. "I've learned that a guy can survive more than he might want to. I've also figured out that our parent's mistakes don't define us. You stayed mad at your dad and made choices about your life because of what he'd done." He caught her eyes with a direct look.

She didn't bother to argue.

Evan's tone softened. "For years I thought God had washed His hands of me."

"Why?" Libby frowned.

"Maybe something I had done? Something I'd said, or even thought?" He scratched his head. "I didn't know one way or the other for sure, but I figured I must've done something wrong."

"You mean because you lost your leg?"

"And my friend on the same day. But that was only part of

it. Getting dumped by Angela reinforced the lies already in my head." He picked up a stick and drew images in the dirt next to him. "I've been thinking about this a long while. I started believing I had to be extra good when I was a kid. I mean, I thought I had to really lay it on. I was the star QB, homecoming king, straight-A student, bronc rider, team roper, you name it and I tried to do it. I tried to do it better than everyone else."

"You succeeded." She sensed they were heading into deep waters.

"There's this one day that really sticks out to me. I know better now, but at the time I was just a kid. I believed when my mom left, it was all my fault and that if my dad knew it, he'd reject me too."

"I think every kid whose parent abandons them believes that to some extent." She had. She'd never gotten along well with Dad.

"Maybe. But see, we all knew Mom was kind of at the end of her rope. She was getting more and more hassled. She yelled all the time, cried a lot, and slept more than seemed normal."

"Sounds like she was depressed."

"Probably. She hated the ranch. This one day, we could see she was already having a pretty hard time of it when we got off the school bus. My brothers were smarter than me and scattered out back. I figured maybe I could cheer her up. I went to the garden and picked all the flowers I could carry and brought them inside while she was upstairs. Then I broke one of her vases when I was trying to fill it with water. I mean, that thing shattered everywhere."

"Oh." Libby flinched.

"Yeah. Not helpful at all."

"You were trying, though."

"I thought I could make up for that by brewing a pot of coffee for her. The pot overflowed. Coffee and grounds spilled all over the counter and floor. I got a towel and started mopping up the mess when our dog puked on the floor. Mom let out a little scream behind me. I turned around, and tears streamed down her cheeks. It scared me."

Evan tossed the stick, startling the hawk. It flew away with the remains of a rabbit in its talons.

"I kept telling her I was sorry, but she covered her face and repeated, 'I can't do it anymore.' She carried on until I was crying, too. Instead of cleaning up the disaster I'd made in the kitchen, I legged it out to the barn. When I finally worked up the courage to come back to the house—around supper time I'm sure—the kitchen was all cleaned up like nothing ever happened. Mom didn't tell Dad. I wasn't in trouble after all, but a couple weeks later, Mom sat us down and told us she was leaving."

"And you blamed yourself?"

"Yeah. Besides being scared and sad, I felt like a coward for not telling my dad and brothers I'd been the one to cause her to go."

"It wasn't your doing. You know that right?"

"I know now, but back then...well, I'd lived with that

feeling of shame until I figured out how to replace those feelings with accomplishments."

Libby reached for his hand. "And thus, Superman was born."

"I guess that's it. I was trying to work my way into acceptance. It all came flooding back when I woke up without my leg. I realized in short order I was no good at anything anymore. Couldn't even take myself to the toilet alone. It took me a miserable couple of years to climb out of self-pity. I believed God wanted me to earn His love, and I just couldn't manage it."

"What do you believe now?"

The corner of Evan's lip curled into a half-smile. "I know that's not true. God has more patience than an earthly parent, and He ain't the type to give His kids the silent treatment. Besides," he said with a wink, "he sent me a fiery little redhead to remind me of my true identity."

L ibby reached across the dry ground for Evan's hand and squeezed. Lightening passed between their fingers, and she let him go like she'd picked up a rattler. Her cheeks were burning, and it wasn't from the sun. Being near Evan emptied her head of sense.

"Mount up, let's head out." Evan threw his weight from side to side in his saddle, making sure his cinch was tight enough. It wasn't, so he dismounted to adjust it. Something that used to be so simple for him was a workout now. He'd have to get used to that.

Libby gave him a quick, apologetic smile. "Remember the pond where our families used to have picnics and fish when we were kids?"

"Yeah." Evan shaded his eyes and pointed." It's just over that hill."

"Right. Let's eat our lunch there."

"Maybe we'll find a toad we can take back in your saddlebag for Theo." Evan teased her with a grin.

"No." Libby tightened the cinch on her saddle.

Theo loved all creatures and his penchant for collecting pets in his pockets had gotten him into quite a bit of trouble at school. Cody had lost more than a few babysitters over it before marrying Molly.

Pulling himself up in the saddle, Evan adjusted his prosthetic in the stirrup and then peered at Libby through his fringe of thick lashes. "Race you there!"

"Don't you dare," Libby warned.

The light in Evan's eyes almost made a race worth it. Almost.

Libby's horse jerked his head, flattened his ears and bunny-hopped sideways. "Oh no you don't. I've been riding all my life, and you aren't getting away with that." She hoisted herself up as Toby tried to crowhop sideways. She swung her leg over the saddle and pulled back on the bit.

Evan was already at the top of the hill by the time she'd gained control of her horse, so she gave Toby the boot, urging him into a canter. Libby grinned into the wind as her hair came loose, whipping her face. She'd missed this country and riding almost as much as she'd missed her family.

After a final stretch with her eyes shut tight, she gathered her reins and pushed her heels down in the stirrups. She leaned over Toby's neck as they climbed the highest point of the hill. "Good boy," she crooned.

Evan was already dismounting when she and Toby topped

the hill. She pulled on the reins and sat heavy in the saddle to slow the buckskin to a full stop.

It was mid-dismount when Evan's muscled arms captured her interest and she nearly fell. He was removing Emmet's bridle, trading it for a halter and long lead. Her stomach did a funny little flip when Evan's eyes flitted her direction. A sharp breath of sagebrush cleared her head. *Keep your mind on therapy goals.*

Evan's balance in the saddle had improved quite a bit. They'd ridden together twice this week. Nice rides where they exchanged ideas about how to help other veterans in addition to the weeklong retreat they'd already planned.

Evan let Emmet graze on clumps of grass, dragging his long lead. He came to hold Libby's reins so she could dismount.

She'd forgotten she was only halfway down.

She hopped to the ground, taking her reins. "Thanks." She switched out Toby's bridle for his halter and allowed him the same freedom as Evan's mount.

"There's shade there." Evan gestured toward a log near a row of poplar trees a few feet from the pond. He pointed out coyote, cougar, and badger tracks leading up to and surrounding the edge of the muddy water. "You're not afraid of cougar, are you?"

"Not with you here." She batted her eyes. "You're bigger and slower than me, he'd eat you first." She giggled when he gave her a mock frown.

"Slower and bigger doesn't mean tastier." Evan sat at one

end of a fallen tree and when she sat beside him, he lunged, tickling her without mercy.

"Stop," she gasped. This was so not appropriate. But the smells of horse sweat, leather, and spicy aftershave collided to cloud her brain.

They wrestled until she gained an advantage after Evan fell off the log. She caught him unaware long enough to give him a rough tickle along his ribs.

His face whitened, he grunted, clenched his eyes, and went still.

Remorse struck when she remembered the bruises along his ribcage. "Oh, Evan, I forgot." She scooted closer when he double over. "I'm sorry. What can I do?"

His hand snaked out and grabbed her waist. He roared and began a fresh tickle assault.

"Okay, I give. I give! You don't taste better than me." She panted.

Evan leaned back but didn't loosen his grip. There was a hard glint in his eye when he arched an eyebrow. "Oh really? Maybe I should check." He closed the gap between their bodies.

Libby froze when his eyes locked on her, asking silent permission. Her nostrils flared in answer.

Evan's lips brushed her chin, her earlobe, her jawline.

She turned her face, breathless, pulse thrumming, to touch her mouth to his. His strong arms came around her, pressing her tight to him as his mouth claimed a hungry kiss. His hot skin left her scorched wherever it touched hers.

Libby broke contact first, eyes pinging up to read his reaction. What was he thinking?

Heavy-lidded and smiling, Evan seemed very pleased with himself. "You're tasty all right. But I'm not sure you're tastier than me. Maybe you should check."

Libby wriggled her arm out from under his and curled it around his neck. His scent and touch befuddled her, but she was past caring. She pulled Evan's head down and nuzzled his throat, inhaling layers of soap, horse, and something singularly male. She sent her fingers to roam the nape of his neck, finding little curls, and teasing them until he made a growling noise and pulled her closer. He kissed her until she was dizzy and lost any sense of time or place. She sighed when Evan dragged his mouth away for a breath.

"You're definitely getting eaten first. You're tastier. I'm sure of it now." He grinned and pressed his forehead to hers.

"You know," she said in a husky voice she didn't recognize, "I probably dreamed of kissing you a thousand times when we were in high school." She played with a soft, brown curl behind his ear, twirling it around her pointer finger.

Evan lifted her up on the log and scrabbled to join her. "I wish I'd known. I thought you were going out with that nerdy kid, Jake Lessman."

"What? Why would you think I was dating Jake?"

"Well…he was the only guy you ever allowed near you, for one thing."

She smiled, remembering the heavy brows and myopic brown eyes behind thick glasses that Jake always wore and pushed up with one knuckle. "We were study buddies, that was all."

"I think he knew I was jealous of him."

"You were not." Libby gave Evan a mock shove.

"Was too. Once when I asked you for help in chemistry class, he caught me smelling your hair. The look he gave me... I wanted to punch his lights out."

Libby laughed. "Poor Jake."

"Poor Jake my eye. Lots of guys were jealous of him, and he knew it. As a matter of fact, I suspect he liked it."

Libby gave him a scolding look.

"Don't try to tell me you didn't notice that dude's swagger during senior year."

"You're ridiculous. You know he had a girlfriend, right?"

"No way."

"Way. They were pen pals. She was from Ellensburg High. They'd met at a debate competition."

"If we'd only known."

Libby smiled and scooted closer. Evan was a better kisser than she'd dreamed. But just to be sure...

Chapter 10

AFTERNOON RIDES

L ate July was hot enough to fry bacon. Evan sat astride Emmet with sweat trickling between his shoulders, waiting for Seth to mount. Libby had begged out of their daily rides until the weather was more forgiving on her fair skin, so Seth had volunteered for trail riding duty. There was a benefit in trading afternoon rides for cooler evening swims.

Libby in her swimsuit.

One thing about Seth, he did everything on his own time. Seth picked up his horse's foot and rested it on his knee. He snagged the hoof pick from his back pocket and scraped the hoof clear of dirt and small stones while keeping his gaze on Evan. "You finally kissed her."

Evan wiped sweat from his forehead and squinted. "How'd you know?"

"It's written all over your face, partner. How long has it

been since you kissed a woman anyway?" He released the sorrel gelding's foot and leaned over the horse's neck.

"None of your business." Evan adjusted his weight in Emmet's saddle. The leather creaked and he made a mental note to oil it later. "When's the last time you kissed a woman?"

Seth laughed and tightened the cinch on his saddle.

"That's what I thought," Evan said. He wasn't ready for the way Libby's kisses made him feel and apparently, he wasn't any good at keeping their new relationship a secret. Not that they needed to hide it but having everyone nosing around in their love life wouldn't be helpful. No matter how well-intentioned their friends and family might consider themselves.

"Not to change the subject or anything, but are you ready for your Wounded Patriot Retreat?" Seth pulled the brim of his hat down lower.

"I have a few interns working the therapy horses. We hired a crew to overhaul the old wrangler's bunkhouse, and I had the stairs torn down to make room for a ramp up to the porch. But I'm not sure the bunkhouse is big enough now that wives and kids are coming. That was Libby's idea."

Seth swung up on his horse.

Evan had started Dusty himself when the sorrel was a colt. That was years ago, before his first tour of duty. Seth had bought him when Evan had been depressed and wheelchair-bound, convinced he'd never ride again, let alone train colts. "Can you convert a barn into living quarters by next year? You mentioned this was a trial run, and you planned to make it annual." Seth smoothed a hand over Dusty's neck.

"I'll figure it out."

Seth jerked his thumb toward a trail Libby had approved for Evan's daily rides. "Ready?"

Nodding, Evan gave Emmet light thigh pressure. It had taken him weeks to build his quads up for that. Libby had helped him tick quite a few goals off his list. He smiled a private smile and adjusted his seat remembering her therapeutic massages on his thigh. She hadn't shrunk back from his implant site. She hadn't even blinked when she touched it.

As they walked a comfortable, quiet pace, Evan's mind drifted back to the last time he and Libby had taken this same trail and ended up rolling on the ground, sharing hungry kisses that made him ache.

"You love her?" Seth's question brought Evan crashing back to the present.

"What?" He nearly choked.

"You heard me." Seth kept his eyes on the path ahead. "She's not like Angela. She can handle it. You know that, right?"

"But does she want to?"

"Libby's tough. And she makes you a better man than you'd be without her."

Evan whipped his head around.

"Look at you. You're in the saddle and even out on trails. I used to think we'd never ride together again."

"I think I do love her," he blurted out. "It's probably too soon to talk like this."

Seth grinned. "You've known her all your life. It's not like you're strangers."

The oily-sharp smell of trampled sagebrush rose from the ground and mixed with the good smells of horse flesh and leather. Evan loved this land. Loved ranching. But would Libby be happy making her life here? They were always focused on his goals. What were Libby's goals? He was ashamed to say he didn't know for sure.

He changed the subject. "Grandpa Smokey mentioned Rose Cameron called him."

Seth let his reins rest across his lap. "And?"

"Your old uncle, Lefty, still lives in the Cameron's house. The one they lived in when Hamish Cameron was alive."

"So?"

"Rose deeded it to Libby. It's her inheritance, but she can't use it while Lefty's living there."

"We tried to get him to move to an assisted living place a few years back, but he flat refused." Seth lifted his hat and rubbed his scalp.

"You know Rose has been paying the electricity bill all these years?"

Seth's face flushed. "I'll remedy that."

"That's not why I brought it up. Just thought maybe we could put our heads together and figure out a solution. Libby's soft-hearted. She won't evict an old veteran."

"Vietnam messed him up. My mom says he's never been right in the head anyway, but I think Lefty's just a loner."

"Well. Let's think on it. The man deserves to have dignity.

I don't think anyone wants to take that from him." Evan lifted Emmet's reins to the side and headed toward the lake. "Wanna race?"

Seth's eyebrows shot up. "Libby would skin me, so no."

Evan shrugged. "Can't have you skinned." Seth was usually game for anything hinting at dangerous, and it got him in a fair bit of trouble. The kid glove treatment was starting to rub Evan the wrong way.

Seth turned to Evan with his head cocked. "It's a noble idea, this retreat. But I thought you wanted to get back to ranching?"

Dusty flattened his ears when they stopped right before reaching a lush patch of grass. "I do. That's my main objective. But I need to give something back. You've heard the statistics on veterans. Homelessness, drug and alcohol abuse, suicide. Something good needs to come out of what happened to me so I can quit brooding."

"My counselor talked to me about all that stuff."

"You see a counselor?" Seth hadn't ever mentioned needing that kind of help.

"I did." Seth's jaw shot out. "I don't anymore, but I needed help to work through some stuff after you came home like you did. Mix in a pinch of PTSD from flying choppers in a war zone and... yeah, I needed to talk to someone." He wiped his hand on his jeans. "You said you have a counselor available to deal with issues that might surface in the veterans coming to the retreat."

Evan eyed Seth. "I do. You never said anything about needing a counselor because of me."

"You had enough problems, and it was only partly because of you that I saw a counselor. My mom insisted in any case."

Evan sucked a breath through his teeth and stared at Seth. A wave of guilt washed over him.

"Bro, you almost died. And then for years, you—never mind. Anyway, yeah. I needed help to deal."

"I was so wrapped up in myself. I didn't even think about you. Guess I've been blind and selfish."

"Don't get all soft and sweaty. I did what any friend would do."

Evan grinned and made a rude gesture. "You're invited to dinner."

"Thanks, but I'm taking Charmaine to the steakhouse."

"Seriously?" Evan gave Seth the sharp-eyed, doubtful look he deserved.

Seth shrugged and looked away.

Evan tried to catch his eyes with a scowl. "You never learn, do you?"

"Apple Valley is a small place. Slim pickings. Anyway, let's do a loop and then get back. Dusty and Emmet are hot."

After a shorter-than-usual ride, they returned to the ranch and handed the horses over to the interns for cooling down before Seth drove away with a wave. Evan headed inside to shower before Libby arrived for dinner.

Molly, the sweetheart, had invited her.

After dinner they had a meeting to iron out a menu with

Salty for the retreat. And Mrs. M agreed to give them an hour as she would be overseeing housekeeping for the bunkhouse. The married veterans were bringing their families, so they'd hired extra help.

"I've planned a light physical therapy session for each morning, and the volunteer counselor will have group sessions at the fire pit in the evenings. That leaves the rest of each day free for fishing, horseback riding, or whatever else they decide to do," Libby said, reading from her notes.

Evan found it hard to concentrate with her hair piled up on her head and her throat on display. He'd kissed her there a few days ago. His gaze lingered on the spot below her ear. He looked forward to catching Libby alone to steal a few kisses in the hallway.

After Salty and Mrs. M asked questions, and made their lists, and left the room, Evan quirked his finger, beckoning Libby to his side of the table. "Come here, darlin'. I haven't kissed you in two days."

Libby set her notebook aside and pretended to consider his request, but she stood fast enough to remove any doubt that she was willing to be kissed. When she stood behind his chair and wrapped her arms around his neck, she dropped a kiss on his jaw.

It only took a second for them to become tangled, but too soon, Libby pressed her hands against his chest. "As much as I'd like to see your eyes get all steamy again, I'm going to have to say goodnight and go on home. I promised to help

Gram with the mailers for the Cattlemen's Ball. I don't want to make her wait because you know how she gets."

Evan smoothed a hand over the silky skin on her arms and felt her shudder. He kissed her arm and tamped down his disappointment. "Let me walk you to the door then."

As they walked down the hall, their hands brushed. His heart did a salsa dance every time they touched. At the door, he snagged her hand and pulled her to his chest. "Thanks for everything you're doing. I'd like to take you somewhere nice for dinner, just you and me, before the retreat."

Libby reached up on tiptoes and placed a whisper-soft kiss on his jaw. "Are you sure you want the whole town to see us together?"

"Who cares?" He pushed a curl behind her ear and stroked her cheek. Her skin was so soft.

"It's not exactly professional for me to be dating someone I'm doing therapy with, Evan."

"Okay," he said with a neutral tone. He hadn't expected her to care.

"I like Mexican food." Libby slipped out the door.

Chapter 11

FIRST DATE FAIL

Libby and Evan rushed through therapy the next morning, so they'd have time for lunch in town. It wasn't quite the same as a dinner date, but with the retreat coming up, they were squeezed for time. Libby looked forward to being alone with Evan away from the ranch and out of the workout room. The only other time they were alone was on horseback and while that was on the romantic side for a country girl like Libby, it still didn't qualify as a date in her book.

Hopping inside one of the Three M ranch pick-up trucks, Libby checked her hair before Evan climbed in the cab on the driver's side. "We only have time for a quick run to town. Lots to do today, cowboy."

"Lunch and home, then?" Evan adjusted the rearview mirror she'd just been using.

"Yep. Mercedes makes the best salsa. Can we go there?"

"Sure thing. Whatever you like."

They drove to town with the windows down and the speakers blaring Tyler Childers. They sang along at the top of their lungs, laughing at Libby's tone-deaf singing all the way to town.

At Mercedes they were seated at a large, center table, the only one available. A server brought them salsa and chips while they waited for cheese enchiladas.

Libby slid the bowl of salsa to Evan's side of the table. She smirked and gave him a sassy wink. "Let's see if you are as hot stuff as you think you are, Superman."

Evan's eyes flipped between the salsa bowl and Libby's face. The gleam that sparked in them matched his daring grin, and a dimple showed in his cheek that made her weak.

Evan took a tortilla chip out of the basket and snagged the saltshaker. He salted his chip and dipped it in the bowl of spicy sauce. The scoop was generous, and Libby lifted her brows to show him that she was duly impressed.

Evan popped the entire thing in his mouth with aplomb, crunched, and swallowed with a smile.

Libby giggled behind her hand as beads of sweat popped out on his forehead, and a flush crept up his neck and into his cheeks.

"Are your eyes watering?"

"No."

"Are you sure about that, cowboy?"

"I'm sure." He coughed and sputtered.

"I think you're lying."

"What makes you think that?" Evan's face was as red as the tomatoes in the salsa. "Cough, cough." He picked up a napkin and wiped his nose, then looked at her and crossed his eyes.

That caused Libby to laugh so hard she snorted. When she could catch her breath and look serious, she picked up a chip, dipped it into the salsa, and slid it into her mouth, making a moaning noise. "So good."

Evan's eyes were watering and sweat was pouring from his forehead. "I can't believe you can eat that kind of heat."

"Oh, buddy, I was made for heat."

When Evan's eyebrows lifted to meet his scalp, Libby's cheeks caught fire. She hadn't meant it like that. She picked up her glass of horchata and gulped. Canoodling in a restaurant, making spicy innuendos whether they were deliberate or not, wasn't her usual style.

A commotion toward the front of the restaurant drew their attention. Gram, dressed in shiny, faux leather pants, an off-the-shoulder black top, and pink cowboy boots waved at them. She pointed Libby and Evan out to Mom and Molly, standing near a potted lemon tree.

"Lib! Mind if we sit at your table? This gentleman was just saying they were out of seats." Molly rushed over and gave Evan a neck hug and then offered the same to Libby. "Cody's watching the kids so we can have a girls-only lunch." She widened her eyes at Evan. "Sorry. We'll make an exception."

Libby lifted her brows at Evan and since he smiled and shrugged, she said yes. There was the inevitable bustle of the trio of women claiming their choice of a chair by hanging a purse on the back and ordering their drinks. By the time the dust settled at the table, disappointment began to nag Libby.

This was supposed to be her first date with Evan.

"Thanks for sharing your table, guys." Molly shot Libby and Evan each an apologetic look.

"No worries," Evan said, sipping his ice water.

Mom thanked their server for her lime margarita and waved her napkin in the air to draw everyone's attention. "Josie's coming home. She says for good this time."

"About darn time." Gram fished a chip out of the salsa bowl and shook salt over it.

Molly and Libby locked eyes and grinned.

"Why? I mean, I'm glad, but what happened?" Molly asked while her thumbs tapped out a text.

"Josie says she's not ready to talk about it, but I'm sure she'll spill the beans at some point."

"Wasn't she dating an Elvis impersonator?" Gram asked.

"Elvis impersonator? Good heavens, Mother. Where on earth did you get that idea?" Mom's eyes widened as if she was scandalized.

Evan hid a chuckle behind his napkin. He pretended to cough, but his eyes were crinkled with suppressed laughter.

"How on earth did Josie meet a man impersonating Elvis?" Molly didn't look up from her phone. Most likely she was texting Cody. Those two still acted like newlyweds.

"She was on a photo shoot for a new line of boots. Very rock 'n' roll type shoot. The models wore black leather and the whole bit. Anyway, she wasn't dating him." Mom emphasized with the sharp point of a corn chip. "The shoot was in Vegas with about a dozen Elvis Presley impersonators. The photos turned out very nice. They were featured in a spread for that cowgirl magazine. I'll show you when we get home."

With a haughty look, Gram dabbed her lips with her napkin. "I'm glad to know our Josie isn't the type of woman to run around with a showbiz type of man."

Molly raised sparkling eyes and turned to Libby. "Do you know the story of how our grandmother kissed Elvis Presley right on the mouth in Vegas in 1971?"

"I did not!" Libby turned to Gram who was busy glaring at Molly and then at Mom. "Loudmouth." She sat straighter and batted her lashes at Evan. "They're just trying to amuse you, dear."

Evan lifted the corner of his mouth and stared into his cup.

Molly was enjoying Gram's discomfort. "I heard this story from Grandpa Cameron's own lips years ago. Gram kissed Elvis Presley during a show at the Imperial Hotel."

No one said a word, but everyone snuck curious glances toward Rowdy Rosie. She seemed to deserve that moniker even more now.

Gram arched a dangerous-looking eyebrow in Molly's direction. "Leave it to you to stir that pot."

"Oh, come on, it was years ago. Besides, you'd think you would want to brag about it now." Molly cajoled, but Gram was looking salty about the teasing.

"Gram? What's the story here?" Libby interrupted the staring contest going on between Molly and Grandma Rose.

"Well? 'fess up, Mother. No secrets in our family, remember?"

Gram's lips were puckered, and she was glowering. "Since you'll all pick my bones clean unless I tell, I might as well get on with it." She pushed her water glass to one side, switching her expression to storytelling mode. She gestured for more chips and salsa and then gave everyone at the table a wicked smile.

"It was 1970. Your dad—" She glanced at Mom. "Had an art exhibit in Las Vegas. You may or may not have known this, but I was crazy for Elvis. I was president of his fan club in Apple Valley. I listened to all his records on repeat." She paused to thank the server for a second basket of chips. "I wanted to see him live in concert in the worst possible way. I hounded Hamish until he promised to buy tickets while we were there for the art exhibit."

Mom snickered and Gram rounded on her. "He saw no harm in it. We made it a family trip. Took my sister and mother along."

"Kind of like the Beverly Hillbillies," Molly said from the side of her mouth.

Mom cleared her throat. "Let her tell the story."

"Anyway, as a gift to me, your grandfather sprang for tickets close to the stage. You know how Elvis liked to come down off that stage and go around in the crowd?"

Molly leaned forward. "You mean kissing all the women?"

Evan was shaking with silent laughter. No doubt he'd get a kick out of retelling this story once he got back to the ranch.

"We never could have guessed what would happen next, but that Elvis Presley, he was something." Gram's voice had gone dreamy.

Mom and Molly rolled their eyes. Libby snuck a peek at Evan who held his stomach, doing his best to keep quiet.

Gram turned up her nose at them. "He kissed two or three ladies on his way to our table—"

Molly lifted her arms in a flourish. "Grandma Rose stood right up for a kiss, and he gave her one too. Right on the mouth, in front of God and grandpa and everybody else"

"I turned my cheek to him," Gram said in a defensive tone.

Molly, triumphant, finished the story. "He grabbed her by the waist and planted a lip lock on her that would curl your hair, according to Grandpa Cameron."

Gram glared. "Who wouldn't want to kiss Elvis?"

"What she hasn't admitted yet is whether or not she gave Elvis her phone number." Molly sat back and folded her arms over her chest.

"Why would she do that? Libby asked.

Gram dipped a chip. "He sent someone around later to ask for it." She popped the chip into her mouth and chewed.

Libby gasped. "Gram! You didn't?"

"Of course not. But I liked to hold it over Hamish's head that I could have."

～

BY THE THIRD day of the Wounded Patriots retreat, Libby was convinced she'd found her true calling. If only she could help combat-wounded vets full-time, incorporating animal therapy.

She nibbled an apricot picked from the tree in the bunkhouse yard and strolled near the bunkhouse Evan had converted for the retreat. Taking out her phone, she made a note to herself about turning part of the grounds into a sort of community, child-friendly garden for the next retreat. They could plant flowers that would attract butterflies, too. She slipped her phone back into her pocket and smiled.

It faltered though when her conscience pestered her about her relationship with Evan.

They should have waited. She shouldn't be seeing a patient. Yet Evan didn't need to be a patient anymore. She'd told him so, and Alex McClure, too, but they asked her to stay on for a few more weeks. She had strong suspicions about their motives. She was getting paid too much to do so little, but they'd insisted the retreat was more work than she'd signed on for.

A child ran past her with a dirty-but-happy face, bare legs, and a pack of ranch dogs. Libby recognized her as the little girl belonging to Steve, a friend of Evan's who had come for the trial week with his family. Steve had lost an arm and the right side of his face. His wife, Trinity, was a beautiful, attentive woman who seemed a bit harried chasing around their other children—three boys in constant motion.

The families gathered at the bunkhouse were an unlikely grouping on the outside, yet they had a terrible thing in common. They laughed a lot and joked about belonging to a club nobody wanted to join.

A man they called Shorty drove by in an all-terrain wheelchair donated to him by the Independence Fund. Libby had seen him giving all the children rides and a few of the dogs as well.

One of the boys she remembered from the first day, Tyler, walked a borrowed goat on a leash, allowing it to nibble bushes and grass. The goat's owner was hoping to rehome it. Libby could only hope Gram didn't get wind of it.

She passed a geriatric broodmare in a small pen and offered her the last bit of apricot in her hand. She was a friendly old girl, chosen to temporarily stay near the bunkhouse for precisely that reason. Callum McClure, one of Evan and Cody's many cousins—an extremely handsome cousin—offered to help with the trail rides for those who wanted them and were capable. "Equine therapy is a big thing, and for good reason. That old mare should really be a help to the kids." Callum had spoken with an expression that made Libby think he really cared. She supposed he did. After all, his cousin had lost his leg in combat.

Evan's family was growing on her more and more. They never flaunted their wealth, which was substantial. She regretted the opinion of them she'd formed in her teenage years. Apparently, she was the snob, not the McClure clan. A little Jane Austin, but true.

Libby had snapped a covert photo of Callum before he left on a trail ride with Evan and sent it to her youngest sister,

Josie. Who knew, maybe that little tumbleweed would stay home for a cute cowboy? As she stroked the mare's neck her phone buzzed a notification. She pulled it from her pocket and grinned. Fish on.

> Who's that?!
>
> Just a cowboy
>
> No, really
>
> He's one of the McClures. I think he's single
>
> Maybe it's time for me to come home for a visit
>
> Whatever it takes!

Her phone buzzed again. Expecting a call from Josie, she moved out of the sun's glare to answer. It wasn't Josie.

"Hannah Pepperidge here, the director for Equine Therapy at Alchemy Ranch."

The facility in Colorado Libby had applied to months before had informed her the position had closed by a curt email rather than a call. It had been her dream job.

"Elizabeth Halverson?"

"Yes."

"Do you have a minute?"

"Sure."

"I know I told you we wouldn't have a spot open until fall, but two therapists left last week without giving notice. We need someone passionate about horses and therapy. You came to mind right away."

"Wow. That's…unexpected."

"I know. Could you fly in next week and start right away?"

Libby's stomach dropped. "That soon?"

"I'd have you here tomorrow if I could. But…paperwork."

"I have commitments right now."

"Okay." Hannah's voice was less enthusiastic. "How soon could you come?"

"That depends." She wanted to protest that she hadn't even accepted the position or discussed contract details. "I'm going to have to get back to you. I'm helping at a retreat for combat-wounded veterans this week."

"Call me Monday?"

"Um. Sure."

She should be happy. She'd wanted that position in the worst way until coming back home. She'd become rooted in Apple Valley, fallen in love—wait. Had she fallen in love?

She had. Libby shook her head.

Molly interrupted her with a wild wave over her head.

"What's up?" Libby glanced at baby Rose clinging to Molly's hip.

"Mom's been trying to find you." Molly wore a Three M logo T with her ashy blonde hair pulled into a loose bun. Her cotton skirt showcased tan legs that ended in cowboy boots stitched with the ranch brand. Ride for the brand had become a McClure family joke since Molly started letting her artistic streak loose on everything she could get her hands on.

"I spent the morning doing Evan's regular PT with him,

and then I did a shorter session with the guests. Is everything okay?"

"Mom wanted to drop off a stack of devotionals from the Books & Brew for the vets along with some muffins."

"That's nice…" Libby was trying to pay attention. Really, she was.

"Lib?"

Libby looked up at Molly and blew out a thin breath. "I just got offered a position I wanted. Alchemy Ranch in Colorado."

"You're kidding?" Molly shifted baby Rose to her other side.

Libby mustered a small smile. "They want me there as soon as possible. I'd have a stable position and get certified in equine therapy."

"But…Colorado?" Molly worried her bottom lip.

"I'll have to think about it. Evan's made so much progress. And there's the Wounded Patriot retreats to help with now. I'm really excited for the potential of this program. I've become passionate about it."

"Why even consider going then? I mean, You and Evan—"

"I know, but I have to earn a living somehow, and Evan doesn't need a therapist anymore."

Molly pressed close to Libby. "Evan really cares for you, Lib, and I know you. You reserved a spot in your heart for Evan only he can fill. You've always wanted Evan, though you're too stubborn to admit it." Baby Rose took the opportunity to grab a fistful of Libby's hair with a slimy little hand and gum it furiously.

Libby extricated herself from the teething infant's clutches. "So did every other girl in this town."

Molly stepped sideways and wrinkled her nose. "Evan isn't interested in any other woman. You're being wishy-washy again." She pinned Libby with cold gray eyes.

Molly was protective of Evan. Libby hadn't noticed before, but it was hard to miss just now.

Crossing her arms over her chest, Libby pasted on her you-aren't-getting-to-me face.

"I know Evan, and he doesn't give his heart lightly. He will suffer if you leave." Molly glared.

Libby blinked hard but tears came anyway. "I'm not sure I should pass on this opportunity. I can't—I don't want to—ever be in Mom's shoes. When Dad left—"

"You're still using Dad as an excuse? You judge him for leaving, but what are you planning to do? How will the kids feel if you go again?"

"I need to have a source of income and this town is small. You have your business, but I don't have the kind of job this town needs."

"Poverty is overrated, I'll give you that. But so is being lonely." Molly gave her a sympathetic look before she spun around the way she'd come. Baby Rose waved 'bye-bye' over her mother's shoulder.

"He's a big horse," said a soft voice at Libby's side, startling her.

She glanced down. Steve and Trinity's little girl stood beside her, staring at the mare in the round pen. She gave the girl a wobbly smile. "Whinny is a lady horse." Libby's insides churned. Wishy-washy? Maybe she was. Was she judging Dad for something she was guilty of? The truth was she tended to change her address when things got hard. It always seemed easier to start over someplace new. Was that how Dad had felt all those years ago? It was no excuse, but it might help her a little if she understood him.

She'd have to give an answer about the job offer. Soon.

The little girl stepped up on the pen rails. She had tousled brown hair falling out of two long braids. "My name is Laine."

"I'm Libby. Would you like to pet Whinny?"

Laine nodded, so Libby called the mare and offered one of the treats she kept in her pocket. The mare nickered and swung her head over the top rail, frightening Laine.

"It's okay, sweetie. Whinny is just excited. She loves horse cookies."

Laine giggled. "Horses can eat cookies?"

"Yep. Horses get cookies, just like kids. These are made from grains, apples, and carrots. Now, want to pet her?"

Laine reached a tentative hand to touch the mare's neck, stroked her, then surprised Libby by pushing her nose into the mare's neck and sighing. "I want a horse someday."

"Laine, come play kickball!" Bella called in a loud voice. "Girls rule and boys drool!"

Theo, along with several other boys stood on a grassy area with scowls on their grubby faces at Bella's taunting.

"You and Bella are the only girls here this week. Guess you should stick together," Libby said.

She was able to laugh at Bella's saucy challenge. The idea of leaving Bella and Theo splintered her heart. But she couldn't stay without an income. And never mind there was still an old man living in the house she'd inherited. Grandma Rose's lawyer offered to evict him, but she'd declined. There had to be another way, but she had yet to find it.

Laine hopped down from the rail with shining eyes. "Thank you." She swiveled and ran to the other children.

Laine's mother, Trinity, drew up to the round pen. She was focused on her daughter. "Laine sure has opened up in the last couple of days. I wish we could stay longer."

"The Three M is pretty great." Libby held out a hand after brushing it off. "I'm Libby, the camp physical therapist."

Trinity took her hand. "I know who you are. I'm Steve's wife."

"It must be a full-time job, being a mom and a wife to a wounded veteran. I admire you. Hope you're getting a bit of a break?"

Trinity tilted her head, and her mouth lifted in a slight smile. "You know, it's amazing what you and the others are doing here. I've had to put on a brave face since Steve came home. It's just that, well, without support and things like this once in a while, it's all so overwhelming. Our lives are one struggle after another."

Libby placed her hand on top of Trinity's. "It can't be easy. Does it ever feel…normal?"

Trinity locked eyes with Libby. "Your nephew has Down syndrome. That won't ever change. Does life with Theo feel normal?"

Libby paused to consider the question. "Yes. He's never been any other way."

"Right. But Steve was. He was a marathon runner. He was the happiest person I knew, and he turned heads because he was handsome, not frightening to look at. Our lives were so different before." A tone of sorrow watered down Trinity's voice. "This is our normal now. We must adjust or fail, and we can't afford to waste time. Steve and I have four kids to raise. He's my partner in life no matter what. He's the father of my kids, and I'm not letting him off the hook." Trinity's voice gained strength with each word.

"From what I can tell, you're doing amazingly well." Libby was no counselor, and she began to sweat.

Trinity's knuckles whitened on the wooden rail. "There was a time...well let's just say Steve was in a dark place. But I went in the dark after him and drug his butt right back to us." She lifted her head. "These guys, they need to feel like men again. Everyone needs a purpose. Those kids—" She pointed to Laine running to catch up with her brothers. "Those are Steve's purpose. With one arm or two, a whole face or half of one, it doesn't change the fact that he's their daddy." Trinity leaned in and said in a discreet voice, "I make sure he knows he's still a man. My man." She looked at Libby hard and then jutted her chin in Evan's direction. He was just riding back with Callum and a small group of guests. "If you decide to join the club that nobody wants to be a member of, then you'll have to be tough, too."

Libby eyed Evan, then turned back to Trinity. "I think I understand what you're trying to say."

"You're smart and kind, Libby. Evan looks at you like you hung the moon." She pushed away from the rail. "I received some very good advice from a doctor once. He told me to avoid the trap of thinking I need to take care of Steve as if he were one of my children. He needs to see me as his woman, not his caretaker." She shoved her hands in her back pockets and scuffed the dirt with her shoe. "Would you accept a little well-intended advice?"

Libby wiped her slick palms on her jeans. This was starting to feel uncomfortable. But hadn't they agreed around the table while planning these retreats that they had to be open to genuine, raw conversations?

Libby met the other woman's large, brown eyes. "Okay." It came out sounding like she felt. Reluctant.

"Don't be his physical therapist for too much longer." Trinity squeezed Libby's hand and walked in the direction of the bunkhouse.

Well and good for her. Trinity and Steve were a married couple with children. Libby and Evan were satisfying their high school hormonal dreams. Did they have the character it took to make the kind of commitment that would last through all the tough stuff life threw down? Were they strong enough to stick even when life tried to split them apart?

Her hand found her phone in her pocket. She had a difficult

choice to make. She could always return to Apple Valley if she left. She had property now, even if she didn't have a clue what to do with it. Or Lefty Hanson, her own personal squatter.

But if she left, she'd be leaving the only man who had ever really taken residence in her heart. Besides Evan, there was her family. She'd missed them like an aching tooth in her solitary years of travel.

Security had been her top priority for so long, she was torn between finally having it and finally having the owner of the dirty old sweatshirt still wadded in the corner of her closet.

"I am wishy-washy," she whispered to Whinny.

Chapter 12

CHEESY EGGS

E van yawned and stretched out in his favorite chair. The downstairs stayed cool during the relentless heat and was the perfect spot to enjoy a cup of coffee alone with Libby.

The picture window with the leather chairs and fireplace had been a sanctuary for Evan during the years when he wasn't quite ready to face the world. Until Bella found him and brought her dolls and books, scattering them on the floor and demanding he feed her babies and read them stories. She'd pulled him back to life by his nose hairs. If only they'd known about her before, not missed her early years

"I'd call the trial retreat a success. How about you?" Libby snuggled in the leather chair next to Evan with a fragrant dark roast coffee. She was gorgeous in a green T-shirt and cut-off denim shorts.

Pumpkin snored like a motor in the doorway. They'd

waved off the last of the Wounded Patriot guests earlier before the sun started baking the ground.

Evan gave Libby a weary but happy smile and sipped his no frills black coffee. "The veterans retreat was everything I hoped, minus a few snags. Thank you for bandaging Gordo's wrist. Your skills come in mighty handy on a rough and tumble ranch."

"Glad I could help. I hope Gordon will be more careful around spooky steers. You'd think he'd know better by now." Libby poured cream into her coffee mug until the dark brew turned light. "Wranglers aren't usually so careless, are they?"

"He's a day worker."

"You'd better rest up for the cattle drive. I remember everyone in the valley having more fun than we should driving the Three M cow and calf pairs." Libby crossed her legs at the ankles. Her hair was loose and a spray of freckles across her nose made her look like a teenager.

"This will be my first year on a drive since I lost my leg. I owe it to you." Evan squeezed Libby's small, soft hand. Remarkable how capable a woman's hands could be. Libby sometimes surprised him with her strength.

"I wasn't going to go if you couldn't. That would be rubbing salt in the wound. I'm excited to finally go on another epic drive. I hope it's like it used to be years ago when everybody saddled up to help."

"Those were more fun than the spring drive when it was just us and the hired men." Evan rubbed his thigh, above the implantation site. It was sore in a good way these days. Sore from riding. That brought a smile to his face.

"Grandma Rose dug out her hat and chaps." Libby's eyes were dancing. He loved it when she got excited.

"Grandpa Smokey made sure to invite your mom and Rowdy Rosey because it's Bella and Theo's first cattle drive."

"Molly's still trying to convince them that their poodles are not suited to cut and herd protective mama cows and their babies." Libby's eyebrows inched up toward her hairline. "Last I heard, Theo was in tears, but Cody put his foot down."

"I should hope so. Those little mutts would get trampled in short order."

"Cody nearly broke down when Bella suggested the poodles could ride in their saddlebags."

"I'm glad he didn't." Evan sipped his coffee and enjoyed the warmth seeping into his being. It was the company more than the coffee.

"I'm hungry. Have you already eaten?" Libby set her mug on the side table.

"Mrs. M is down with a head cold, so I settled for coffee here." They were all a little worn out after the retreat. "Salty might have leftovers from the cowboy's breakfast."

"Mrs. M worked too hard all week." Libby raised her auburn brow.

"I ordered her flowers."

"Thoughtful." Libby's face softened with approval. "I hear Salty's a fair cook."

"Mostly, but he ruins a good farm egg."

Libby's dark gold lashes framed eyes the color of the ocean. "How so?" she asked.

"He cooks them until they're rubbery." Evan shifted his weight to his other hip. "I don't remember a lot of things my mom cooked when I was a kid, but I do remember her cheesy eggs, and I miss them."

"Cheesy eggs, huh?" Libby uncrossed her legs and tucked a loose strand of hair behind her ear. "My mom makes cheesy eggs on Christmas morning. Grandma Rose taught her and my aunt Olivia when they were so young, they had to stand on chairs to reach the stove. Mom taught us girls. I'll bet it's the same recipe because your mother used to go on the big campouts before she... anyway, we always had cheesy eggs, sausages, and biscuits over the campfire. Do you remember?"

Evan smiled. "How could I forget?"

"Do you ever hear from her? Your Mom, I mean."

"Just on holidays. Guilt I expect." Evan shrugged. Mom wasn't a sore point anymore. They'd had a few good talks when he'd been in a rehabilitation center after his first two surgeries. He'd grown up hearing from Dad and Grandpa Smokey that holding a grudge was like poisoning your own well. "What idiot would drink that water every day?" Dad would ask when Evan and his brothers were younger and feeling the loss of her especially hard sometimes. Like birthdays, Easter, and Christmas.

"People don't get together like they did in the past." Libby's lips turned down.

"No. They don't. Besides, when our grandparents started

becoming elderly and we lost your grandfather and my grand-mother, the old folks lost heart for those gatherings." Nostalgia crept into his soul. "I'd like to revive some of that." He missed their large families all crushing together, blending into one. Before Afghanistan, he thought he'd be married with kids by now, keeping those days alive for the next generation of ranchers.

"Let's start with cheesy eggs this morning. I can make them," Libby volunteered, perceptive and kind as always. She wasn't nearly as tough as her reputation suggested.

"I'll admit that watching you cook one of my favorite dishes might do things to my heart," Evan said.

A blush bloomed on Libby's face, but he glimpsed the small smile she tried to hide. She uncurled like a cat from the chair and padded barefoot to the small kitchen. Her hips swayed in a way that held his eyes prisoners.

Pumpkin yawned from the doorway, stretched, and padded into the kitchen. Her ears drooped when Libby shooed her back out.

"Come here, Pumpkin Girl. Sit." Evan stroked the dog's head as a small compensation.

Libby sang softly while she rattled in the cupboards for a pan and then took butter, cheddar cheese, and a bowl of eggs from the fridge. Generally speaking, this was an extra kitchen, not Mrs. M's domain, but she kept it stocked for the odd guest or for the rare times she went away from the ranch. Salty had a commercial kitchen in the basement as well as an outside kitchen with a spit for roasting meat. He fed the wranglers and interns and on occasion, the household. Molly had treated them to some fine dinners on Mrs. M's night off before little Rose came along. Evan hadn't cooked anything aside from toast his entire life.

Thinking of Molly and the kids got him pondering about how nice it was to have children in the house. He'd never thought to ask Libby if she wanted them.

Libby scrolled on her phone and was soon swaying to Pop music while shredding the cheese. The scene was so domestic, so exactly what he wished for every morning, that a lump formed in his throat. He tried to swallow down the longing, but it only grew when Libby started singing in a tone-deaf voice.

He pushed out of his chair, debating a clumsy attempt at a slow dance when the song changed. He missed dancing but he didn't think he could manage it. He had a week to go before he'd lose his bet with Libby. There was no way he was going to be able to do the two-step by his Alive Day. Maybe she'd forgotten, but his conscience would pester him if he didn't own up.

"Do you like regular cheese or extra, Evan?" Libby stopped shredding and turned to face him.

Evan cleared his throat and found his voice. "Extra cheese, please."

One brow flicked up. "Good. Me, too." She looked at him a long moment before turning back.

After taking in the view for a few minutes, he walked into Libby's work area and leaned on the counter. "Can I help?"

"Absolutely. Crack those eggs, Superman."

Picking up an egg, he cracked it into the glass bowl Libby pushed his way. He repeated the process until he had half a dozen eggs in the bowl, bright orange yolks floating in a clear, albumen sea.

Libby took the bowl without looking at him and added a splash of milk and whisked the eggs like a tropical cyclone.

"Poor eggs," Evan remarked.

Libby looked up and laughed. "Now add some butter to the pan, will you?"

Evan added a pat of butter. Libby turned the dial on the burner, set a pan on the stove, added the egg and milk mixture, and stirred with a rubber spatula. She cleared a path on the bottom of the pan at every turn. "I forgot to grab the salt and pepper. Would you sprinkle the eggs while I stir? You know I can't stop, or they won't cream properly."

He salted the eggs first, deferring to her for the amount, and then added the pepper. She liked quite a bit. Evan nodded in approval. Just the way he liked them, too.

"Now the cheese," she said, pointing to the mound of sharp cheddar waiting to melt over the eggs.

Evan scooped the cheese up with both hands.

"Sprinkle it a little at a time," Libby bossed him with a happy lilt. She stirred the eggs with a heart-bruising smile on her lips. She seemed completely content making their breakfast.

"That's starting to look amazing, and now I'm really hungry." Evan's voice came out as a growl. He was hungry for more than eggs.

Libby's brows rose and her lip curled in a knowing way. She chuckled and focused on the cheesy eggs again.

Evan leaned over to sprinkle more cheddar then burrowed his nose in her neck.

Libby let out a little squeak but stretched her neck to offer her throat. She shuddered and Evan closed his eyes, inhaling the warm scent of vanilla on her skin. "Mmmm. Delicious."

"They will be. They're almost done."

"I'm not talking about the eggs."

Libby left the spatula in the eggs and turned into his chest. She kissed the cleft in his chin. She had no idea what she was doing to him. Or maybe she did. She bumped him away with her hip and a beguiling smile. "Better watch out, cowboy. You might give me the wrong impression." She spooned a portion of eggs into a bowl and set it aside to cool. "For Pumpkin," she informed him.

Evan sprinkled the rest of the cheese with one eye on Libby's face. How could she be in doubt about his feelings? "What impression am I giving you?"

"That you like me quite a bit," she said without hesitation.

"You know that I do."

"But we haven't really talked about it, have we? I mean, we've known each other forever. We've kissed...held hands, but we never actually—"

Evan tipped her chin up and closed her mouth, kissing her until she stood on tiptoes. "Hopefully that communicates plenty."

"Evan, I've been offered a job," she blurted the words. "A facility in Colorado needs a physical therapist."

He took a step back. "When did you find this out?"

"Grab two plates and let's get these eggs off the heat or they'll be as rubbery as Salty's eggs."

Furrowing his brow, he brought two plates, forks, and napkins to the breakfast bar. Libby spooned the eggs onto the plates, giving him a larger portion. She set the pan on the butcher block cutting board, refilled their coffee mugs, and then finally sat down next to him.

Evan's fork was poised to lift a bite of the perfectly creamed eggs and cheese, but he wasn't at all sure they'd go down now. "Okay." He set the fork on his plate and pushing it aside. "Let's talk first and then eat."

She shook her head. "Eat first or they'll be cold, and all that work will be for nothing." She pushed Evan's plate in front of him.

Evan picked up the fork. "Can we eat and talk?"

Libby sighed. "I suppose."

Evan forked his first bite of the eggs and a flood of childhood memories burst into color. "Perfect, Lib."

"They are good, aren't they? We make a good team, Superman."

"Are we a team?" He tried to stop the pleading tone in his voice but knew he hadn't succeeded.

"I've thought of us that way," she admitted. But her face closed, and he could feel her edging away.

Evan reached across the table and brushed a strawberry-gold curl away from her face. He stroked her cheek tenderly with his thumb.

Libby's eyes were pained when she looked at him. "I need to work, and I'm not convinced I can make a living here like I'd hoped."

The fluffy eggs turned to lead in his gut. Life would go back to gray without Libby. It wasn't that he'd come to rely on her for rehabilitation. He'd slipped up and come to rely on her smiles and more recently, her kisses. "You can get another job here. I mean...you're the best. Your reputation alone should make it easy to find another position."

Libby's mouth pulled into a weak smile. "Thank you for trying to build up my confidence, but Apple Valley is a small town. There's only one clinic and every position is already filled."

Evan took a fortifying sip of coffee. He was chasing a future he thought he'd lost—and he'd come to think of Libby in the center of it. "Can you continue to do private pay?"

"You won't need me for too much longer. Then what? I have to work." Her tone had a bit of starch.

What could he say that might influence her to stay put in Apple Valley? It was far too early to say out loud what his heart begged for.

He lifted his eyes and she lowered hers.

A chill swept over him and suddenly, this moment seemed too familiar.

How could he let himself believe Libby would be the one woman who would stay?

Chapter 13
PEACH PIE PICNIC

Evan was quiet for the rest of the week. Too quiet. But what had she expected?

Libby rinsed her coffee mug and set it upside down to dry on the draining board. Evan had texted her early that morning to say he had a business meeting with his family, and he'd do his therapy on his own later.

The truth was—he didn't need her anymore.

Maybe once a week, certainly not every day. Her employment at the Three M Ranch was about to end. The thought pained her. She'd come to love the ranch. She enjoyed the teasing and banter of the cowboys and seeing her sister and the kids so often. The lodge was big enough to get lost in, but somehow, she wasn't intimidated anymore. It had become familiar and even cozy.

Libby had put off giving Hannah Pepperidge an answer about the position in Colorado, but the woman was getting testy over Libby's lack of commitment. Apparently, there were no other likely prospects, or the position would have been filled by now. She'd prayed and prayed but had no sense of peace about taking the job. She'd moved back home because of feeling lonely and rootless. She didn't want to move to Colorado, or anywhere else.

But with Lefty Hanson in the house she'd inherited, she'd have to live with Mom and Grandma Rose in this farmhouse—the unofficial old ladies' clubhouse.

Inspiration struck as she considered what to do about Lefty. The old veteran must be lonely. As a bachelor, he'd likely welcome company. Especially if that company came with peach pies. Maybe some chicken salad sandwiches and Mom's homemade dill pickles...

The front door slammed shut and Gram's corgis roused themselves to rush the entryway and bark.

"You stop that." Gram used the voice she meant to scald ears and strike terror. The dogs obliged her and tucked their tails all the way back to their oversized bed under the living room window seat.

Libby dried her hands on a dish towel. "Need help carrying anything?" She padded out of the kitchen on bare feet.

Gram was a sight in hot pink yoga pants, and oversized Rodeo Quincy T-shirt, and brand new, white cowboy boots. A full shopping bag clung to her shoulder, but just barely and the wild rag on her forehead was lower on one side. She looked like she did after coming home from a Black Friday sale in Prosser, the closest actual city with decent shopping.

"Here, let me take that. Where have you been?" Libby took the bag and peered inside.

"Don't be nosy."

"Don't you already have a closet full of boots?" Libby set the bag down and hitched her hands on her hips.

Gram rolled her eyes. "As if there were such a thing as having too many boots. You could learn a thing or two from your sisters." She held the wall while she struggled out of her new purchase. "Take those out of the box, please." She lifted her eyes to meet Libby's. "You could do with bigger earrings. Look great, feel great, I always say."

"I feel great without hula hoop earrings."

"What are you doing home, anyway?"

"The McClure men have a team meeting, so I find myself with a day off. I was just thinking of making some hand pies to take over to Lefty's house. Maybe I can become friends with him."

Gram's head snapped up. "You mean your house, don't you?"

"Well, I guess it is. I'm trying to find a solution that won't leave Lefty homeless. What do you say to helping me make some hand pies?" She fixed a sugary smile on Gram and prepared to flatter her. "Nobody equals your flaky crust."

"Well, that's true enough. Put those boots in my room, and I'll wash my hands."

"We have a whole box of ripe Alberta's from Johnson's Orchards."

An hour later, the kitchen was fragrant with the warm

scents of peach, pie crust, butter, and a fresh pot of black raspberry tea. Gram was dusted in flour and wilted in a chair waiting for well-deserved refreshments. Libby poured fragrant tea for her and placed the reward of a still-warm hand pie on a Spode dessert plate, Gram's favorite Blue Italian pattern. She kissed her fluffy, white head. "Thank you."

Gram nodded and set a cloth napkin in her lap. She took a sip of tea, and her entire body seemed to revive. "Coffee in the morning and tea in the afternoon. We've raised you right, young lady. Now, you'd better get on with your preparations to win over Lefty."

Libby frowned. "I thought it would be nice to have a cup of tea with you."

"Another time. You have a date with destiny just now. Hustle up and don't miss it." She bit into her pie and rolled her eyes heavenward. "Delicious." She swallowed her bite. "Make sure you take one to Evan."

Libby caught Gram's wink over her shoulder.

After searching out the picnic basket, assembling some legendary sandwiches, and adding a pint jar of Mom's pickles —which she had to sneak out of the pantry—Libby was ready to go. She called to Pumpkin.

"I prayed for you," Gram called from the doorway as Libby drove down the dirt driveway in her Jeep. "Get your house back!"

Arriving at the old homestead that used to belong to her grandparents but now belonged to her—and Lefty, unfortunately, Libby checked out the house and property. She'd expected it to be more rundown. The house could use a fresh coat of paint, but the lawn was mowed and Grandma's old roses, well-pruned, still bloomed, filling the air with perfume. The fence had fallen in places but that was easily remedied.

Stepping out of the Jeep with the picnic basket, she practiced a friendly smile. "Stay here, Pumpkin. I'll leave the windows down, but you'd better not try to get out. I don't want you chewed up by Lefty's dog or shot."

There was a loose board on the porch but otherwise it looked recently swept clean. A pot of dark purple peonies stood as an elegant welcome on one side. "Nice touch." She whispered just in case Lefty's dog came to tear her vocal cords out for trespassing. She smoothed her skirt, knocked on the door, and stood back, clutching the basket to her chest.

The door opened and dark eyes peered at her from the crack with squinty-eyed distrust. "Yes?" A voice like gravel questioned her.

Libby smiled wider, then cleared her throat. "Lefty Hanson?"

"Who's asking?"

"Libby-er, Elizabeth Halverson. Rose Cameron's granddaughter."

He stared.

"We haven't seen each other in years, but I—"

"I remember you. And I know why you're here." There was hostility in his voice and upon further inspection, it matched his expression.

"I just came to talk today. Really. Well, also to ask you to have a picnic with me." Libby fanned her lashes. Her cheeks were heating up. The curse of being a redhead.

"A picnic?" There was the tiniest glimmer in his eyes.

Libby took advantage of that. "You remember my grand-mother's award-winning pies, don't you? I've brought you a few peach hand pies and some of my mom's dill pickles, too."

Lefty's nose twitched while his eyebrows inched up toward his thinning hairline. "What else?" He opened the door wider.

It was hard not to be obvious, but Libby snuck peeks inside. The living room furniture was mismatched but every-thing looked orderly and wonder of wonders...clean. "I made chicken salad sandwiches, too."

"Do you drink tea?" He stood aside. It was her invitation.

"Yes, please." She stepped into the house—her house—and was wrapped in the scent of wood polish. The staircase leading to the bedrooms upstairs was gleaming. She hadn't been inside this house for years.

"Kitchen's this-a-way."

Libby followed him obediently, even though she knew perfectly well where the kitchen was. "It's nice in here."

"Surprised, aren't ya?" Lefty laughed in a way that sounded more like a bark. Which reminded her...

"I thought you had a dog?" She swiveled her neck around. She didn't want to get bitten.

"I did. She passed on last winter." His voice was sorrowful.

"I'm sorry."

He shrugged and pointed to the kitchen table. It was covered in a floral cloth bunched up on one side to make room for a sewing machine. Libby stared at it and then up at the old man.

"Regal was old. I miss her, though I'm grateful she went peacefully. Went in her sleep during her afternoon nap. Guess her old heart just quit."

"I have a dog," Libby ventured in a tentative tone. "Pumpkin. She's out in my Jeep."

Lefty narrowed his gaze in a judgmental sort of way. "It's too hot to leave a dog in a car."

"Well, can I bring her inside? With us?" It couldn't hurt to try and maybe, just maybe, Pumpkin would soften his crusty exterior.

"Suit yourself."

She sat the picnic basket on the table and went to get Pumpkin. She glanced behind her and smothered a giggle. Lefty was going through the basket like a kid sneaking cookies from a cookie jar.

Pumpkin was wagging her tail when Libby opened the front door for her to come inside the house. She sniffed around a bit then headed straight for Lefty in the kitchen.

"She likes you," Libby said.

Lefty's eyes grew misty. He sat in a chair and invited Pumpkin to sit beside him on the floor. She gave him adoring looks while he patted her. Libby would give Pumpkin extra treats for putting her best paw forward. She eased into a chair and unpacked the basket, filling up the two plates Lefty had placed in the center of the table. They were mismatched but clean. An old tea pot, chipped and cracked, steamed with Earl

Grey. Libby inhaled with appreciation. It was Grandma Rose's favorite.

Lefty took a plate from her, poured tea into a John Deer tractor mug, and offered it to Libby. She took it with a smile. Things were going a thousand times better than she'd dared to hope.

"Cream?" he asked.

Nodding, Libby pulled an old ceramic cow creamer to her side of the table and gave it a sniff test when Lefty wasn't looking. It was cream all right. She splashed some into her mug and then sat back and fixed her face into a hopefully friendly expression. The man was suspicious of her no matter how badly he wanted the contents of her basket.

"I'll save you the effort of telling me why you're here and just say it. I ain't leaving my home."

Heat flushed Libby's face. "But the point is, Mr. Hanson, this isn't your home." She'd be respectful no matter how agitated he got. She knew how to deal with veterans feeling distress. She was a threat to him. She'd just be calm and reasonable.

"Mr. Hanson is it now?" He shook his head and gave a scoffing laugh. He spoke to Pumpkin rather than Libby. "Trying to kick me out of the homestead after ten years of me keepin' it up, are they?"

"No. That's not…I mean, my intentions are—"

"Save it for the judge."

"Judge? What do you mean?" Was this old man crazy? This was her property.

"Squatters have rights in Washington state. Everybody knows that." He tilted his head in an arrogant way that said he thought he had her beat.

Maybe he did.

"Let's don't talk about this today, okay? I just wanted to get to know you and let you get to know me. We have a problem, and if we work together, maybe we can come up with a solution that we both—"

"You mean, you have a problem."

Libby picked up her mug and took a sip. She didn't care that it burned her on the way down.

"Look, little lady. I got nowhere else to go. I'm stayin' right here."

"Another pie?" she asked with a bit of asperity. When he shook his head, she closed her eyes and asked the Lord to help her.

When she opened her eyes, Lefty was feeding bits of chicken salad to Pumpkin from his plate.

"Lefty?"

"Hmm?" he didn't look at her but was all smiles and sweetness for Pumpkin.

"I rescued that dog. She was scheduled to be put down."

"What's your point?

"I just wanted to show you that I'm not a heartless person."

"Goody gumdrops." He crossed his arms over his chest. "I won't be persuaded."

She'd try another angle. "You must get lonely here." She scanned the kitchen, her eyes roaming the sparkling clean windows. They landed on the sewing machine. "Are you making curtains?" The man was full of surprises.

"I do get lonely." He smacked his lips. "But Seth and some of my other kin visit now and again." He pinched another morsel for Pumpkin and let her lick his fingers. "And yes, those are curtains. What of it?" He rounded on her with a defensive tone.

"I'm impressed, that's all. I've never been terribly domestic myself." Mom always said you caught more bees with honey than vinegar.

"Must be why there's no ring on your finger." He gave her a dismissive look and took another sandwich.

It required most of her willpower not to snatch the sandwich out of Lefty's hand. "Maybe you're right. Do you give lessons?"

Lefty met her gaze with a startled expression. "Lessons?"

"Yes. Sewing lessons. Maybe you could help me get a ring on this finger." She waggled her ring finger in front of him. "While you're teaching me, we can come up with a plan that will satisfy us both about this house."

"Rosey called me. Said you'd inherited the old homestead and she was sorry, but I'd have to move."

Libby lowered her eyes at the anguish in his face. "I'm sorry, Lefty. I really am."

"I won't go to that old folk's home, and I'm too old to sleep under the stars."

"Let's leave it for now. We'll think of something. I promise I won't try to make you go unless you decide you want to."

Lefty's small eyes blinked back tears. He stroked Pumpkin when she put her paw on his leg. "She's a good dog."

Tender-hearted by now, Libby blinked back a few tears of her own. "She is."

What could she do? People didn't just give their inheritances away, did they? Besides talking Lefty into becoming roomies, which wasn't in the great ideas category, she was at a loss for how to navigate the predicament Gram had placed her in. Gram was good at stirring pots.

Oddly enough, it was her visit with Lefty that decided her. She belonged to Apple Valley and everyone in it, and they belonged to her. Lefty needed help. She didn't know how, but she would start praying about it right away.

Her whole life she'd relied on herself for security, but she'd been believing a lie. Just like Evan thought he had to be spectacular for God and everyone else to love him, she'd believed she had to do everything on her own.

She called Hannah Pepperidge and declined her offer. She would have been thrilled to get the position a few months ago, but from now on she was going to trust God, even when it didn't seem prudent.

Chapter 14
A GOOD RANCH HAND

E van was saddled up for a ride with Libby and sweating before they'd even started out. Seth was busy, so Libby had agreed to brave the heatwave. An awkward distance had slipped between them since Libby told him she'd been offered a job in Colorado. He missed being close to her. Missed touching her soft skin and kissing her.

Evan laid the reins on Emmet's neck and slipped leather gloves on.

Libby tugged on the cinch of her saddle. She lifted her boot into the stirrup and hoisted herself up and over the back of a tall sorrel gelding. The wrangler who brought him out of the pen for her said the horse's name was Bill. A retired cutting horse and all-around ranch horse, he was calm and level-headed. Today was a test to determine if he was a good fit for the Wounded Patriots string of horses.

Libby lifted her face to the sun, and Evan stole a glance at her from under his hat brim. The freckles across her nose made him consider nudging his horse close enough to kiss them, but he wasn't sure how she'd react. He cued Emmet to move up and give Bill and Libby room on the trail.

"How's the left side?" Libby asked.

He put weight in the stirrup on the prosthetic side. "No pain at all."

"Good." She gave him a prize-winning smile. "I went to visit Lefty."

"Oh?"

"He refuses to leave, but I can't blame him. I don't know how to sort it out yet." She shrugged and made a kissing noise to Bill. He obliged for a few steps then slowed down again. "He's a perfect beginner's horse."

Evan chuckled.

They walked on a bit and the slow, undulating motion of his body on horseback under the sun made Evan feel boneless. Libby, too, seemed relaxed. They were silent and so were the birds, usually deafening in the orchards this time of year. Must be the heat.

The doctor told him he'd soon feel the prosthetic touching ground, almost like sensations of a limb. That day couldn't come soon enough. The cattle drive was coming up and it just happened to land on his Alive Day. There would be music and dancing that night at the camp.

Would Libby be around for the Cattlemen's Ball next month? He hoped to dance the two-step and win their bet. She'd agreed to go as his date if he did. She'd been closed-mouthed about the job offer, and he hadn't worked up the courage to ask.

Libby clicked her tongue, and Bill perked his ears and continued his sedate walk. "Let's go through the pear orchard and follow the trail to the river. The cattle in that field are tame, right?" Libby was smoothing Bill's mane to the correct side of his neck while she talked. It was clear the horse had been left out to pasture for some time, but he seemed willing to please even if he was as slow as a snail.

Evan readjusted his prosthetic foot in the stirrup and nudged Emmet to the path Libby had suggested. The sound of the horse's hooves on the dirt were hypnotic and comforting after a few moments. The air had a fresh scent from the wild-flowers they trampled along the path.

His family had owned this land since the mid-eighteen hundreds. He was proud of the history handed down detailing how each generation managed to keep it. Maybe, just maybe, he was beginning to feel he was going to contribute something to the McClure legacy, too. He reflected as they rode. He'd been a cocky youth, never doubting his abilities until only part of him came home from war. Then he'd spent a few years doubting everything— mostly himself.

They dodged pear tree branches as they rode through the orchard. Emmet's hooves squashed overripe pears rotting on the ground and stirred up hornets. The air was syrupy with the pears' scent here. They came to the end of a row and startled a hawk on the ground standing on its prey. It spread impressive wings and took flight over their heads, brown rabbit dangling from razor talons.

There was nothing better than a day spent in the saddle.

Libby rode ahead when they reached the end of the row into a wider part of the path. She leaned over her saddle and unlatched the gate to the field, rode through, and waited as Evan followed. He reined Emmet to the side, latched the gate, and grinned at their accomplishment. He could never fall for a woman who didn't know the rule about gates. If you found it open you left it that way, and if you found it latched you latched it behind you. Libby'd make a good ranch hand. Or wife. On a cattle ranch, those were essentially the same thing.

"Did I mention I decided to turn down the position in Colorado?" Libby acted casual when she dropped this bomb.

Evan tugged Emmet's reins and stopped in the middle of the trail. "You did?"

"Mmmhmm." She kicked Bill to a rough trot, but it only lasted a few paces before he slowed down again. Libby swiveled in the saddle, resting her hand on Bill's big rump.

Evan trotted Emmet beside her. "Do I dare say, even though it sounds selfish, that I'm relieved?"

"Me too, cowboy. Now, let's ride."

Evan gave Emmet his head and smiled into the sky to see if his heart was floating up there.

Libby was staying.

They meandered through fifty acres of good field grass before they spotted a group of black Angus cattle. They were newly bred and meant to be getting fat on the high, rich grass all summer. Libby lifted herself in her saddle to stand in the stirrups and raised one hand to shield her eyes from the sun. Evan pulled up and scanned the hill below them.

"It's kind of ridiculous that my job is going on trail rides on a huge ranch with a handsome man." Libby reined her horse close enough to hook her finger through Evan's belt loop. Bill's ears flattened as she kneed her him closer still and angled her head to reach Evan. "Kiss me, cowboy."

Evan blinked in surprise but leaned over the pommel and pressed his mouth to hers. The unfamiliar horses got into a scuffle and moved apart.

"Do you see that?" Libby pointed to a low area with a clump of sagebrush. "Be quiet for a minute...listen."

Evan cocked his head and sniffed the air. "Birth scents. And I hear a cow bawling."

"I thought you said these were young cows, newly bred?"

"Supposed to be, along with a few too young to breed that the interns let get mixed in."

"Well, I see a bull. Look at that red blob in front of the clump of sage down there."

"What the...you're right." Evan squinted and rode forward for a closer look. "Dad's not gonna be happy about that." He kicked Emmet and they rode down the hill. "That's not the McClure brand on that animal's hide. We'd never breed such a mangy critter. The red Angus and Herefords are in higher pastures. But generations of cattle have been lost out here and formed their own herds. Anything's possible."

"He's got someone else's brand." Libby pointed. "He's from another local herd."

They both wheeled around in their saddles when the noise they'd heard a moment before sounded again, more urgently.

"I'll call in the bull and let the wranglers deal with him. We'd better go see what's happening in that sage. Stay behind me." Evan rode in the direction of the distress call and then stopped twenty feet from the brush. He climbed down from his saddle with his rifle. He held Bill's reins for Libby while she dismounted.

"Oh, poor thing. I think the calf is stuck," Libby whispered. She kneeled in the dirt to stroke the neck of a young cow, eyes bulging with panic and pain.

Evan nodded brusquely. "She's too young. We need to pull it, Lib. Do you think you can help me?"

"I think so." Libby bit her bottom lip, resolve in her expression.

Yep. She'd make a good rancher's wife.

Evan squashed that thought. She would, but for a rancher with two legs who wouldn't need his wife to take care of him.

The flirty kisses between them should probably stop. That painful dart shot all the way through his heart in the time it took for him to untie his rope and pull down his saddlebag.

He didn't want to stop kissing Libby. Ever. She looked at him like a woman looked at a man she wanted. Fragile ego aside, he was in love with Libby.

Evan pulled in a hot breath of trampled sage and blood and fixed his mind on the job in front of him. He walked toward the little cow. She was laying on her side, moaning. "She's given it a good try, but she's tired," he said in a soothing voice. He bent down and stroked her shoulder. "Libby, go to the back end of this beast and tell me what you see."

Libby walked around and squatted. "I see a nose and two feet, but they are poking back in every time she strains."

"That's good. Real good. Okay now, you come pet this girl and talk sweet to her. I'm going to pull that big sucker out."

They traded places and Evan removed his T-shirt, wiped the front feet of the emerging calf dry, wrapped them in the cotton shirt to give him a better grip, then leveraged himself with his prosthetic foot on the cow's rump and his other foot anchored into the rocky soil. "I'm gonna pull, and she isn't gonna like it. You sit on her neck if she starts to get up."

Libby shot a nervous glance in his direction. "Okay."

Evan gripped his hands around the two legs and pulled. The cow hollered, and he pulled harder. She was resisting him now, he could feel it, so he stopped. "Put your hand on her side and nod when it goes hard."

Libby placed her hand on the cow's side with a frown. After a moment her eyes widened, and she nodded.

Evan pulled for all he was worth, and the calf popped out with a gush of fluid, landing in a soft, wet pile between his legs. He worked fast, pulling the shirt free and wrapping it around the snot-slippery back legs so he could lift the calf up. He swung it gently until it snorted fluid from its nose and bawled. He grinned and slid it in front of its mama.

"Get aquatinted with your little bull calf," he encouraged

the new mother with a soft tone. She didn't move so he nudged her with the toe of his boot. Her eyes flew open, and she lifted her head and sniffed the calf. Evan let out his breath when she began to lick him.

"Instincts always kick in, don't they." Libby scooted close to the calf and spoke soothing nonsense to his mother. "Good thing Superman came riding along, huh girl?"

Evan straightened and wiped his hands on his jeans. "Any rancher would do the same. I've been pulling calves since I was five."

Libby laughed. "Probably true, but I'll bet the miracle of birth still touches you. I know it does me." She tilted her head to look at him, and his heart leapt into his throat.

She'd never looked more beautiful. She wore a smudge of dirt—or something else—on her cheek and had a slimy calf draped over her lap. His heart reacted to the sight like a rabbit with a pack of dogs chasing it. "Be careful girl, or you're gonna make me fall in love with you."

Libby caught her breath, flustered. She snatched Evan's discarded T-shirt from the ground and wiped the calf's nose and mouth. Love? Did Evan say the L word? Heat scorched her cheeks. Her pulse stampeded, but Evan seemed oblivious to the effect his words had on her.

"That's for sure a little bull calf," he observed after lifting one slippery leg to peer at the creature's underside. He took the shirt from her and dried the inside of the calf's ears. Their hands brushed and their eyes met, communicating so much neither had the courage to say. At least, she didn't.

Evan hoisted the calf from her lap and gently placed it under his mama's nose again. "She needs to clean him by herself so she can bond and memorize his scent. Out here, his survival depends on her."

Libby nodded and offered a tremulous smile in his direction. She wanted to say something. To tell him she was falling in love with him too, that maybe she'd been in love with him since Sunday School class. They'd spent nearly every day together for months. He couldn't possibly doubt her feelings. Could he?

But if she spoke her feelings, they'd have to be acted on. Words were powerful. "I love you" were words she'd only ever spoken to her family, a dog, and maybe two horses she'd owned as a kid. She'd never said them to a man, because once outside of her they couldn't be taken back.

Was she ready to receive those words from Evan? To offer them to him?

He'd spoken lightly, but after their shared kisses and tender smiles she felt sure he cared for her. He wasn't one to play with another person's heart. She knew him well enough to know he wasn't careless with others. Only himself.

The sky was changing from shades of blue to melon and soon it would turn to lavender and charcoal. They should head back.

"Wouldn't it be nice to be like our great-great-great-grandparents, just setting foot on this land and deciding to settle and build a cabin just there?" Evan pointed to a stand of ancient trees casting shadows over a stream leading to a small pool of sludgy water. There were a few head of cattle drinking from the pool and more at various points along the stream, heads down and throats bobbing as they drank.

"I think I'd choose a spot right in the middle of the meadow so I could have sunlight in all the windows," Libby said.

"That would be nice. But back then they worried about enemies, predators, and bad weather. If you look at one of the original cabins across the lake, you'll see only one window and it isn't a big one."

"Grandma Rose says Grandpa told her stories about his grandparents. His favorites were about the cabin window."

Evan held out his hand to lift her to her feet.

She took it, rising with a groan. She'd sat too long, holding the newborn calf.

"What stories did your grandfather tell about the window?" Evan licked his thumb and rubbed at something across her cheek.

If she were a teenager, she'd probably vow to never wash that side of her face again. She laughed at herself.

Evan cocked his head. "What's so funny?"

"The small window had a shelf where my great-great grandmother cooled her pies after pulling them from the wood-fired oven. Grandpa liked to tell the story about how every once in a while, he and his cousins would get so impatient for a piece of pie after dinner that they'd sneak under the window and steal a whole one. They'd take it to the woods and polish off every crumb. Then they'd have to leave the plate somewhere, of course. So, they'd plant it over by a black bear's den so she would blame the pie theft on the bear. That seemed fair to them since the bear sometimes did steal a pie and never got caught. But then one day, Grandpa Cameron said their grandmother had had enough."

"What happened?"

"Well, the kids heard their grandmother cussing a blue streak. They ran around the back of the cabin, hiding in her lilac bushes to see what she was going to do about that stolen pie. They were wide-eyed and shaking when she marched toward the woods. Grandpa figured if she got eaten by that bear it would be their fault. They loved her, so they followed close behind even though none of them had any idea how to fight a bear to save her.

"That big black bear was standing up on its hind legs eating wild plums from a tree near its den. Grandpa Cameron said she saw the bear, then her pie plate, and her face turned the same shade as the plums. She ignored the bear, walked right up to the den, snatched her plate, and backtracked to the bear. She was like a tornado, and he swore the bear was frozen with fear. She got right under its nose, called it some terrible names the kids weren't allowed to repeat, then took one step back. She hauled off and smacked the surprised bear with the pie plate he had supposedly stolen."

Evan threw his head back and howled. "What did the bear do when she hit him with the plate?"

"Grandpa said the bear let out a bellow, ran off toward the woods, and must have changed his address because he was never seen in those parts again."

Evan wiped his eyes. "Something tells me you have some of your great-great grandmother in you."

"Of course, I do." Libby huffed. "Our ancestors had to be tough to settle this land and bring in cattle, water, fruit…"

"Don't I know it. I'm afraid Old Smokey might be the last of that tough breed. The rest of us McClures are softies compared to him."

"Oh please. You're called Superman for a reason. And I remember the way you broke colts in high school. Cody rode bulls in sixth grade for crying out loud."

"Then there's Nate living on the road with a rock band. Our grandmother would have cried herself to sleep over that boy if she were still alive."

"Nate will come home and settle down. He's just tasting his danger off the ranch. Don't look at me like that, Evan McClure. All of you men get a kick out of living dangerously."

Evan shrugged with a self-deprecating grin. "I hope Nate comes back to the ranch soon. I'll never be as capable as I was before losing my leg." Evan's face darkened.

"Maybe. But lots of cowboys ride four-wheelers now. Your father even uses a helicopter sometimes."

"Machines aren't ideal. They stress the animals more than horses and men."

"Is that why you're so determined to ride every day?"

"Partly. And partly because I could never imagine my life outside of ranching. This dirt holds the DNA of us McClures. Unlike Nate, I never wanted a life away from the Three M. I'm proud of what all the men and women in my family have built. Cody and I have always wanted to protect our western heritage, our way of life. We always wanted to pass it along to future generations." He flicked his eyes away. "Of course, we'd like Nate here, too. I pictured the three of us boys with our wives and kids keeping this land for another couple generations at least…but Nate left, I got blown up and never married…"

"You almost did. I mean…Angela."

"I was young and dumb with hormones. Ranching is a hard life, and if Angela couldn't stand by me after I lost my leg, she sure wasn't going to stand by me through a lifetime of raising cattle and horses in the summer heat and the winter snow. Ranch life isn't for everyone." Was he thinking of his mother?

"The ranch house isn't exactly rough living. Molly feels like a queen in a log castle." Libby smiled.

Her beautiful sister was living her best life after struggling as a single parent in New Mexico. Molly had hidden her pregnancy from Cody when he'd returned from the rodeo circuit with a pregnant buckle bunny on his arm. He'd no idea Molly was pregnant, too. To Cody's credit, he cowboyed up and married Theo's mom because he thought it was the right thing to do.

Libby had always thought Molly should have told Cody as

soon as she saw those two pink lines on the test, but then maybe they wouldn't have Theo in their lives. God redeemed bad situations. Molly and Cody were proof.

"Look, Libby. The calf." Evan nudged her. "He's up and nursing."

Libby wiped her hands on her jeans, but they weren't any cleaner than her slime-covered hands. She turned her head to see the expression on Evan's face more clearly.

Her stomach fluttered at the tenderness there.

Her masculine, tough guy could be so gentle. Evan had managed to reverse the bad taste her father had left her with. She'd grown up in Apple Valley, a town full of swaggering cowboys that took the time to carry groceries for their grand-mothers—or anyone else's grandmother—as well as stop to rescue stray dogs and drifters. She never should have held on to her bitterness and disappointment surrounded by such good men.

Evan turned a heart-wrenching grin her way, and her insides melted into warm butter. He might only have been joking about falling in love with her, but she was falling for him and this time it wasn't just a schoolgirl crush.

Chapter 15
CATTLE DRIVE

Libby loved living in a small town where farmers and ranchers helped each other. Neighbors were often nearly as close as family. But nothing brought together a ranching community like a cattle drive. Today, everyone but Molly and the baby would join the work and the fun.

Mom sat in Grandpa Cameron's old saddle, fresh-faced and sparkly-eyed. She reined her buckskin mare to stand next to Grandma Rose's old Appaloosa gelding. Theo and Bella were showing off new, custom chaps on their tall ponies. They'd started out on Shetlands, but Cody had upgraded them last year.

Evan rode up front on Emmet. Seth Hanson sat astride a horse named Dusty on the left flank of the herd. Cody and more of their relatives rode with Smokey, flanking the herd on the right side. The McClures seemed prone to having sons. Libby lost count of uncles and male cousins.

The rest of their party was made up of half a dozen cowboys and several local ranchers who drove out with their horses in trailers to help. A few long-faced interns hung back with instructions to keep up the daily ranch chores.

Libby was on a level-headed bay named Snickers. He was a low to the ground, fast on his feet, gelding. "Very cowy," Evan had declared when he brought the bay out to her. She was thrilled with his choice, but even more thrilled at Evan's sure, steady gait as he walked back to Emmet. Libby stroked Snickers' neck while she enjoyed the rear view of Evan's Wrangler jeans. He'd gained muscle over the weeks and balanced his lower half. He wasn't as top-heavy as before.

Bella and Theo trailed Mom, who looked great in a denim shirt, a tank top, and a wild rag protecting her throat. She was western through and through, even if she was a bit vain about her skin. Gram was the caboose in turquoise boots that were far too expensive to be on a cattle drive. Eccentric. That was Gram.

Libby would love to own a horse again, but that's not what she was longing for right this minute. She hid a smile and snapped a picture of Mom on the back of the buckskin. In Aviator sunglasses and a baseball cap to protect her face from the sun, no one would guess that Mom was in her fifties.

"You look like one of my sisters rather than my mother. I hope to see you dancing with the cowboys tonight," Libby called to her.

Mom lowered her Aviators and winked.

"You look the part of a cattle puncher today, but I hope

you've got mineral salts for when we all get home in a couple days." Libby adjusted her Three M logo hat.

"I ride for the Three M most years, and so does your grandmother." Mom jerked a thumb behind her back. "You're the one who isn't used to a full day in the saddle." She reined her buckskin in a tight circle when the mare snorted and laid her ears back at Snickers. When her mount settled, she pointed to Libby's hat. "I like that look."

"Thanks. I got it from Ross McClure," Libby returned Mom's teasing. Mom and Evan's uncle had flirted and turned red in one another's presence for at least ten years. "Evan told me Ross's crew will be working the rear flank of the herd this year. You know," she added with a wicked grin, "just in case you find yourself needing to stop and pick out a stone from your horse's foot or something."

Mom shoved her sunglasses back up and kicked the mare toward the front line of cowboys.

Libby laughed when Smokey pointed her back to the tail, gesturing for her to stay with Bella and Theo. Smokey was the drive boss, and nobody crossed the boss on a cattle drive. Mom rode back with a poker face, but Libby would bet she was glaring at her behind those mirrored glasses.

Snickers stood quiet in the midst of the chaos, resting on his right back leg and swatting flies with his long, black tail. "I've missed this," she whispered. The horse's ears flicked in acknowledgment. She could do this every day for the rest of her life.

"Move out!" The command came from Bertie Valdez, the

Three M Ranch's cattle foreman. The dogs got excited, barking, and running around nipping cattle to begin the trek to a lower pasture, near natural springs.

Although she couldn't see his eyes behind his sunglasses, Libby's skin tingled where she could feel Evan's watchful gaze on her. She smiled in his direction and reined Snickers to the left side where she'd been told to watch for straying cattle. The first hour was just a steady walk in the direction of the hills. They'd flushed a herd of wild horses that had been on the McClure land for decades. She was thrilled to spy three leggy new colts in the herd. Evan had told her that Smokey set his wife's mare free to live with the wild horses after she'd passed on. It was a romantic notion. Maybe one of the colts was a descendant of that mare.

"Pay attention to your job, Lib. You've let a pair run off into the trees," Grandma Rose admonished her with an accusing finger jabbing her direction. Her red hat was pulled low, but Libby caught the glint in her eye as she jostled closer. "Chase after 'em, girl. Don't dawdle, either."

Libby tugged Snickers' reins and squeezed his sides. He stretched his neck and cantered after the mama cow and her calf. They dodged around a stand of trees, and Libby found she only needed to give Snickers his head and let him do his job. He flattened his ears and stretched his neck until he could reach to bite Mama cow's rear. She kicked her heels and swerved around a boulder. The calf, losing sight of his mama bawled as it veered in the opposite direction.

Libby sighed. It had really been too long since she'd done

this. She had her doubts about being able to rope the calf. The noise of the herd moving ahead, the dogs barking, the cowboys whistling, and the calves bawling, receded.

Great. Now she had accidentally cut this pair out of the herd.

No one had seen them aside from Grandma Rose and who knew if she'd turn around to check.

Libby swiped the sweat from her forehead with the back of her hand and wiped it on her jeans. The cow had run off in one direction while Snickers and the calf stood staring each other down. Every time the calf tried to dodge them, Snickers anticipated it and jumped to that side. Libby grabbed the saddle horn, squeezed her thighs, and was just about to utter a prayer when she spotted something in the tree line.

Make that several somethings.

Snickers snorted. Libby tried to urge him closer, but he side hopped and tossed his head. He rolled his eyes, danced, and snorted. Libby kept turning him in circles while she scanned the tree line. Wolves? No, these were several different colors.

A low growl came from one of the creatures as it stepped forward, followed by four more.

Dogs.

Her stomach hollowed and ice zipped down her spine. Packing dogs were dangerous predators. Two more dogs came out of the trees. A German shepherd, several mixed breeds of various sizes and colors, and a large, matted brown dog with yellow eyes and bared, yellow teeth. They all crept forward, eyes glued to the calf. They growled, menacing Snickers who was losing his mind. It was all she could do to keep the horse from bolting, but she couldn't leave the defenseless calf to be torn apart by the pack of dogs.

A bellow and pounding hooves came from her left side as mama cow charged, head lowered. The dogs snarled, and while half their number came to worry the cow, the rest pounced on the terrified calf. Snickers reared, eyes rolling, his sharp hooves striking at a dog. The horse tried to take the bit between his teeth. Libby wasn't sure she could—or should—force Snickers to hold their ground. It was dangerous for them both, but she couldn't abandon the mama and her baby. Especially since it was her fault they were alone and vulnerable.

With one hand gripping the reins for all she was worth, she used her other hand to wave around while she shouted at the dogs. If only she had the pistol in her saddlebag. She'd left it in her Jeep, not wanting the extra weight.

The dogs attacked the calf, biting him, and before Libby thought better of it, she spurred Snickers into the fray. He pinned his ears, reared, kicked, bucked, and made noises Libby felt in her bones. This wasn't her horse to endanger but her instincts overrode sense. She kicked out with her boots, connecting with a huge, black dog who howled in pain, but recovered himself in an instant.

This wasn't working, there were too many dogs.

The large brown dog lunged at Snickers and tore at his nose. The horse shrieked and reared, causing Libby to tumble backward and land hard. The fall knocked the wind from her so when she tried to scream, she didn't have enough air.

Just when the mangy brown dog lunged at her and she figured she was a goner, shots rang out. Dogs scattered in all directions. Libby rolled over and curled into herself, burying her face in the dirt, with her eyes clenched shut. More shots, then something grabbed her shoulder.

Libby screamed then. She screamed and screamed.

"Shhh, Lib, it's me. It's Evan. You're okay. I'm here." He wrapped an arm around her waist and helped her sit upright.

The calf was trembling on the ground with his mama standing over him, shaking, dripping blood and slobber. A brindle dog lay crumpled a few feet away, dead, she hoped. A huge yellow dog was laid out on the ground, and a trail of blood smeared the rocks and dirt where the others must have taken their leave. Snickers was gone, but so was the pack of dogs.

"You're a good shot." Her voice sounded far away with her heart thundering in her ears.

Evan's hands trailed over her body, his brow furrowed in concern. The expression on his face was savage.

When his hand pressed over her right arm, she winced. "Painful?" he questioned her with a gentle voice.

Libby nodded. "I think so. I don't...I don't really know. Is the calf going to live?"

Evan tried to straighten her arm to feel along the bone.

She cried out, pulling it back. It was already swelling with a purple bruise. She tipped her head and met Evan's worried eyes. "It's broken," she said.

"Nope, but it's pretty banged up, sweetheart." Evan palpated her shoulder. "I think you're in shock. Just lean your back against my chest, Libby. I'm sure someone heard those shots."

"Okay." She began to quiver all over.

Evan wrapped his arms around her, and she let herself melt into his broad chest. She was safe.

A low growl made her tense. The alpha dog had its evil, yellow eyes locked on them. Where had the mongrel come from? Those narrowed orbs darted to the calf and struggling mother, then back to Libby and Evan.

Evan tensed too. He slid his arm behind him, pulled his pistol from his belt, and steadied it on his target. "Press your ear to my chest. I'll cover the other one before I shoot, okay?"

Libby nodded, mute. Evan's large hand radiated heat as he covered her ear with it, crushing the side of her face into his chest. She held her breath and waited. Where were the others? Where was their help? She whispered a prayer, then cracked open an eye. They were still in a stand-off with Cujo. She prayed for protection, and just as she'd mouthed a silent amen, a shot rang out and the brown dog dropped.

LIBBY STEPPED out of the tent she shared with Mom. She was saddle-sore and her arm throbbed, but her heart was light. The music had started, and the aroma of a wood fire and roasting beef tantalized her empty belly. Gram and the kids had already changed and were in line for their well-earned supper.

Libby trailed Mom, scanning the crowd for Evan.

"Imogene, over here!" One of the serving ladies held a huge spoon in the air and waved it in Mom's direction. Mom waved back and left Libby alone in the supper line to go chat with her friend.

Libby smiled as she greeted old neighbors and answered questions from concerned ranchers about the number of dogs she'd counted in the pack. She'd expected Evan to join her but when she reached the front of the line, he still hadn't shown up.

"Evening, Miss Libby. I heard what happened today. You sure you're okay?" Salty looked her over while he forked smoky beef onto her plate.

"I'm fine. Just got a bit rattled. Besides, every now and again a little danger is good for the soul, right?" She smiled at the cook.

Salty shook his head. Libby moved down the line and chose a warm, golden roll before moving to the side dishes. She answered similar questions all the way through the serving line and had to grin at the extra helpings foisted on her—country mamas did like to reward a person with food.

Libby resigned herself to eating without Evan's company and found a recently vacated flat rock to sit on. The juicy beef tasted even better than it smelled. Working outside all day tended to sharpen a person's appetite.

Evan's dad took her by surprise when he came around from behind her rock with a fistful of wildflowers. "You saved two valuable animals today. It's not much, but I'd like to thank you." He set the flowers down beside her.

"Thank you, they're beautiful. But the truth is, it's my fault the pair were apart from the herd in the first place." Her cheeks got warm. She'd been negligent of the duty assigned to her.

"Not at all. Happens to the best of us." Alex's expression was so warm, she believed him. "Don't let one incident put you off. You were brave today, and I'm grateful. However,"— he gave her a tight smile—"please don't risk your neck like that again. No cow is worth your life."

"Yes, sir." Libby dropped her gaze to her half-eaten plate. "Did Snickers get stitched up?"

Alex nodded. "All fixed and given extra oats. That horse sure proved his worth today." He dipped his chin to acknowledge a couple of wranglers passing by. "Evan will be around any minute, I expect."

Libby's head snapped up. "I was wondering..." she didn't finish her thought, seeing laughter in his eyes.

"I'd better get a plate before Salty runs out of roast." He tipped the brim of his Stetson and headed toward the food tables.

Appetite gone, Libby set her plate aside and swayed to the music, keeping an eye out for Evan. The cattle drive was only half over, but the first night the McClures always had a to-do for their crew and helpers. She'd forgotten how much fun hard work could be when it was a community event.

The hired band began a cover song that was perfect for dancing the two-step. Today was Evan's Alive Day and it was the perfect day to let him win a wager. She meant to hold him to the bet he'd made with her back in May.

The band's lead was singing the lyrics, "You're the one I need," when Evan, in a fresh, long-sleeve button up and clean jeans, caught her eye.

She sent him a look she hoped stirred his blood. She was ready to dance.

He gave her a heart-stopping smile and motioned her to join him. "Let's get some pie." Evan led her to the dessert table. "Apple, berry, or peach?"

"One of each?" She stood and dusted off her rear.

"My kind of girl." Evan planted a smiley kiss against her mouth. "Care to share?"

"Sure."

Pie was well and good, but she'd hoped he was going to ask her to dance. She had no doubt he meant to make good on their bet tonight.

He added a generous slice of each kind of pie on offer to their communal plate while Libby collected napkins and forks. They wandered to a vacant table, set up for the party by Salty and his crew while the rest of them had been driving cattle. And battling a savage pack of dogs. Evan set the plate down and came around to pull the plastic chair out for her.

"In case you haven't guessed by now, I've fallen pretty hard for you, Lib."

Libby stopped chewing the morsel of pie crust she'd

snitched from the plate. She dropped her hands to her lap and pinched herself under the table. Her heart was doing something ridiculous and mildly concerning inside her chest. Hadn't she longed for Evan McClure to say those words to her? It was hard to believe he'd dropped them so casually. "Evan, I—"

"There you are, Libby," Smokey McClure's deep, gruff voice startled her. "That wrangler sitting on his back pockets over there in the dirt hurt his ankle doing some fool jig of a dance. Can you see to him?"

Stomach sinking, Libby dropped her napkin on the table and nodded. "Sure." She met Evan's eyes across the table.

He gave her a wink. "I'll wait here unless you need help, darlin'."

She followed Smokey to the lanky cowboy who'd perhaps had a bit too much hard apple cider and pulled off his boot. He hollered and sobered real quick. She probed his swollen ankle. "I think it's a bad sprain. You'll have to get it seen to be sure. Stay off it until you've had x-rays." She patted his knee. "Looks like you're going home in the morning, cowboy."

Alex, standing next to Smokey, motioned for Libby to join them. "Get some ice on that ankle, will ya, Shane?" A lanky teenager from a neighboring ranch nodded and jogged toward one of the coolers.

"Libby, my father and I've been thinking on something for a couple of weeks."

"Oh?"

"A ranch as big as the Three M, with so many injuries

every year, could do with a permanent physical therapist, on-site, so-to-speak."

She took a moment to process the words. "I'm not sure that would be worth your time. So many days might go by before I was needed. There isn't always an injury to deal with." Did Evan know what they were discussing? She craned her neck around, but Evan was getting serious about those pies.

Smokey studied her. "My other sons also have ranches, and they'd be grateful for your services, too. You'd split your time between the three spreads." He smoothed his beard and squinted. "We'd provide a ranch truck for you, of course."

"Is Evan aware that you're offering me a full-time position?" She glanced between the two men.

"No. But I can't imagine he'd mind his girlfriend sticking around the ranch." Alex's meaty hand landed on her shoulder. "You don't have to give us an answer straight off. Think on it some. We'd like you to be sure in any case."

"Get back to one of us soon, though. I'm tired of having to drive injured cowboys to town. 'Sides, when Doc orders 'em to do therapy, I lose two men. It takes another to drive them into town for appointments. You'd save us money in the long run."

Libby grinned and stuck out her hand. "Sirs, I'd be proud to work for the McClure ranches as resident physical therapist. No more thought needed. In fact, the job is an answer to prayer."

"A handshake and a smile. That's how deals are done in Apple Valley. What's goin' on here?" Grandma Rose rose to just below Alex's chest, but with her hands on her hips, she embodied authority.

"Rosey, meet the Three M's newest full-time employee." Smiling lips peeked from under Smokey's mustache.

Grandma Rose turned to Libby. "God works fast sometimes." The twinkle in her eye indicated the whole thing was probably her idea.

Libby nodded. It had been a full day. She was itching to get back to Evan. Her mind played volleyball with his words, and her pulse was still skittering. "I look forward to working with your crews." She shook hands with both men again and excused herself.

Evan was waiting.

Chapter 16

REVELATIONS & REDEMPTIONS

E van considered the dwindling pie in front of him. They could always get second helpings. He savored the peach pie with the hope Libby would come back before he'd eaten the whole slice. He was going to give himself a belly ache. What was taking her so long?

He leaned back and cut his eyes to the cowboy Libby had gone to tend. He was sprawled on a log with his leg stretched out in front of him, a bag of ice across his ankle. By the look on his face, his head was as sore as his ankle. Libby's attention was on Dad and Grandpa Smokey. Now, what were they jawing about?

Lingering on the pleasant view of Libby's sweet smile and the way the sun caught a gleam in her hair, he wished he could read lips. He couldn't, so he forked another bite of Sherry Sutherland's peach pie into his mouth and chewed it slowly. His mind was playing the what-if game. It was starting to upset his digestion, so he wiped his mouth and pushed the pie plate away.

What if Libby had been mauled or even killed by those dogs? The sight of her tossed like a rag doll onto the rocks with a snarling dog about to tear out her throat had been more than he could handle. He'd acted on reflexes, and thank God, he was still a good shot, because his true aim wasn't due to practice.

The Almighty had guided his hand.

One thing became clear—he couldn't do without Libby. The way she'd looked at him after he'd rescued her, completely trusting him for her safety…well, it did something for his manhood. When she was most vulnerable, she'd shown him her heart. He was sure of it, and he meant to be worthy of her. She'd given him his life back with prodding, pushing, and a stubborn refusal to give up on him. Or allow him to give up on himself.

He loved her.

Evan pushed the pie aside and stood. He was going to interrupt the monopoly Dad and Grandpa Smokey had on his lady to swing her around the dance floor and win a bet. And hopefully, her heart.

"Evan?" A tentative hand on his arm accompanied the familiar, tentative voice.

What was she doing here? Before meeting Angela's eyes, he examined his heart.

Nope. Nothing. Good.

Relieved, he faced her. "Hey, Angela." He pushed his

hands into his pockets and cocked his head sideways. "I don't mean to be rude, but I'm surprised to see you here." Or at all.

Angela's eyes skipped around nervously.

"I-I know. Maybe I shouldn't be. But I have to say something I should have said a long time ago. And I can't...I just can't go through with tomorrow until I talk to you." She pressed a wilted tissue to her nose. "I don't know if you heard—"

"I had. Congratulations on your engagement to..." he searched his memory for an answer.

"Donnie. Donald Silverman from Pasco." She sniffled.

"Can't say I've met him."

"No, you wouldn't have. Evan..." She tore at her bottom lip with her little sharp teeth. Her eyes were round as saucers, pleading with him for something. "I told Don about us and explained that I can't say our vows at the church tomorrow until I've apologized to you. I know words won't cover it, but...but words are all I have."

Evan no longer needed her apology, but it was nice to know he hadn't completely misjudged Angela's character. He held out a hand. "Apology accepted." He met her eyes so she might see his sincerity.

A small sob escaped her. "I'm so relieved."

"I hope you have a good marriage and a happy life." He meant that.

Angela dried the tears sneaking down her cheeks and smiled a sad smile. "You always were a generous man. I'm sorry I wasn't as strong as you needed me to be. I failed you.

The truth is, I would have failed if I'd stayed, sooner or later. I'm just not as strong as you are." She took a step back and sniffled. "Look at you!" She swabbed at her puffy eyes again. "You're walking and riding. Next thing, you'll be out on that dance floor."

Evan glanced at the group milling around in front of the band. "I set some goals for myself, and I mean to knock out one more of them tonight. I made a bet after my last surgery that I'd be dancing the two-step by today." Of course, he'd made that bet with Libby, and had every intention of winning it with her. But somehow, Angela showing up to say she was sorry on his Alive Day just seemed providential.

"I know I wronged you, and tomorrow is my wedding day, but what do you say to one last dance? I may not have been able to keep my promise to you, but I'd like to help you keep one to yourself." She looked up from under damp lashes. "A tiny bit of redemption, I suppose."

Evan held out his hand, and she took it.

The band struck up a Josh Turner cover and suddenly, they were dancing. Quick-step quick-step, slow-step slow-step, quick-step quick-step, slow-step slow step. Evan was stiff on the left side, but he managed. The song was fast-paced, and he'd stumbled a bit, but he and Angela laughed over it. They danced the whole song. When it ended, Evan raised their clasped hands over their heads in victory. Everyone clapped and cheered.

"I'd better go," Angela said. She was breathless, and Evan

wondered if maybe this wasn't the kind of apology Don had in mind. Word got out in a small town.

Evan led Angela out of the circle and walked her to her car. "Thanks for the dance. It meant the world that you came here to talk to me." He opened her door. "You'd better get yourself home, now. Don is sure to wonder if you've run off with cold feet." He hadn't meant that to sound like a dig, but the way she widened her eyes…

"He knows where I am. I came with his blessing."

"Good. Well…"

"Goodbye, Evan. I hope you find a woman who is everything you need. Have an amazing life, you deserve it."

He watched her drive away with gratitude that the Good Lord didn't always give a person what they thought they wanted.

LIBBY STOPPED to check the swelling on the now-sober cowboy's ankle. He'd be hurting in the morning by the looks of the purple band around the swollen joint. She sent him to his tent to elevate it with the help of another cowboy.

The table where she last sat with Evan was empty, so she scanned the clusters of people for his tall frame. Maybe he'd gone to see how Bella and Theo were getting on. But no, they were with Mom, their faces stained with berry pie. Libby waved. She'd tell everyone else about her new job after she shared the news with Evan.

Cheers and clapping drew her attention to the couples dancing in front of the wooden platform some of the cowboys had nailed together that day for the band.

The sight of Evan and Angela together stopped Libby's heart. How was it possible? She rubbed her eyes. Had she hit her head when she tumbled from her horse?

No. It really was Angela. And she'd never looked better. Her eyes were shining as Evan lifted their entwined hands in the air. The face-splitting smile of victory he wore ripped a hole in Libby's lungs. She winced at the pain.

People were cheering for Evan because he'd danced, not because he had his old fiancé back. Libby pinched her hand, reasoned with herself, but her emotions refused to be reined.

Evan's hand slipped around Angela's shoulder and then the backslapping began. Friends, neighbors, and relatives stepped up to high-five Evan. Libby should be proud that her work had helped another patient succeed. But Evan wasn't just another patient, and her betrayed heart couldn't see reason. It was her own stupid fault. She knew better than to fall for Apple Valley's Golden Boy.

Still, that was supposed to be her in Evan's arms. That was supposed to be her two-step.

"Honey?" Mom dipped her head to catch Libby's eyes and slipped an arm around her waist.

Libby couldn't look away from Evan and Angela. "I can't believe it happened again."

"What do you mean?" Mom's voice was soft. She tucked a stray curl behind Libby's ear.

Libby turned away. "High school all over again." She gave a brittle laugh. "Angela has a talent for swooping in right under my nose." She pulled away from Mom's embrace and headed for her tent.

"Libby? Come back, please. I'm sure there's an explanation. I happen to know she's getting married in the morning."

Libby snorted. "I feel sorry for her husband."

Inside the tent, she stuffed the few things she'd brought on the drive into her backpack and zipped it so hard the zipper broke. She needed to put some miles between her and what she'd just witnessed. But what was she going to do? She was in the middle of nowhere and she'd ridden a horse here.

How could Evan do it? How could he toss her aside the minute Angela showed up and crooked her finger at him? It hurt to breathe.

That dance was important. Monumental.

And he'd shared it with Angela instead of her.

Jerking the tent door aside, she stepped out, swung her backpack on her shoulder, and headed for Salty's crew. They'd driven here with the food and coolers. She marched to him, ignoring Mom's voice.

Salty stood with his beefy arms crossed over his chest and shook his head. "Sometimes you need to look at what's just past your nose, Miss Libby."

"I'm not asking you for relationship advice. I'm asking for a ride back to the ranch. My Jeep is there."

"We don't go back to the Three M until late tomorrow morning. Sorry."

"What?" Libby touched his departing shoulder. "Please, Salty."

"We're camping here. I can't spare any of my crew neither, so don't ask." He scowled. "We serve a big breakfast at four a.m." He took a step sideways. "Goodnight. I'm headed for my tent."

Libby glared at the cook's back. Tossing her backpack on the ground, she looked over the camp and considered who might let her catch a ride back to town. The band? Maybe. But she'd have a long wait.

"Libby?" Evan's voice rose above the music. She peered into the firelight from the shadow of a tree. He couldn't see her.

Taillights in the distance meant she'd missed an opportunity to leave with someone. She searched the crowd but didn't see a trace of Angela. Were those her taillights?

Mom was pointing Evan in her direction. Great. She didn't want to talk to him right now. Or ever. She glanced behind her. It was too dark, and that way led to the cattle herd and perhaps lurking dogs. She stifled a hysterical giggle. Maybe she could ride one of the cows home. That's something Grandma Rose would do. Her giggle snagged on a sob. Pressing her hand over her mouth, she ran for the trees. She needed privacy to sort things out.

She stayed in the shadows and circled around to the far side of the campfires, where people were roasting marshmallows and telling stories. Bella danced with Cody while Theo dozed in a lawn chair near a fire. A burnt marshmallow dangled from the end of a stick drooping from his hand. Libby gently pried the marshmallow stick from her sleepy nephew's hands. She should help him to his tent.

A rough hand on her arm made her swing around. "Dawson?" One of Evan's cousins grinned at her but the look in his eyes was shrewd.

He jerked his chin toward Evan, limping their way. "Care to dance?" The look he gave her! He knew. Who didn't? Libby's cheeks burned.

Taking the hand Dawson offered, Libby followed him to the center of the makeshift dance floor. The band played a slow song. Gritting her teeth as Dawson's hands locked on her hips, she swayed with him. When she met his eyes there was a glint she didn't like. He'd always been in competition with Evan. This was his moment.

Evan stood with his arms hanging loose, watching with a frown. Libby turned her face into Dawson's chest. This must be what it was like to dance with a brick wall. She'd never liked Dawson, he was arrogant and had broken the heart of every girl dumb enough to date him.

Libby's spine stiffened when Dawson winked down at her. Seems the McClure men had more than a few things in common. The music ended, and Evan came toward them quicker than she'd seen him move before. She stepped back from Dawson and his overpowering cologne.

Dawson pulled her in for a quick hug, then stepped around her. "Thanks, ma'am." He reached into his pocket, pulled out a wad of cash, and stuffed it in Evan's fist.

"What's this for?" Evan had steel in his voice and more in his eyes.

"Old wager. Remember our high school bet concerning Miss Libby Halverson here?" His top lip was curled in almost, but not quite a sneer. "The guys were all talking about it a few days ago. We agreed that you won." He slapped Evan on the shoulder. "Thanks for letting me dance with your girlfriend. Course, you were busy with Angela anyway." With that parting shot, Dawson sauntered away.

Evan clenched his fist around the money, looked down at it, then eyed Dawson's back and started toward him. Libby put a hand on Evan's forearm. She shook her head.

Evan tossed the money on the ground. "Libby, I've been looking for you. I wanted to explain—"

"You don't have to explain a thing. I saw you."

"I know. Your mom told me, and I think you mis—"

Libby held her palm out. "You can dance with whoever you want. You're a grown man with no attachments." Libby turned on her heel and left Evan standing alone.

She wasn't about to let him make a fool of her twice.

Chapter 17

IMPULSIVE IDIOT

E van's stomach gave him fits through the night and the whole next day. Libby wouldn't talk to him. She'd refused to look at him or hear anything he had to say. The stubborn woman was determined to be angry at him.

She rode away from him every time he tried to approach her for the rest of the cattle drive. After that they'd been so busy sorting pairs and administering vaccines and freezing brands that he hadn't found a chance to get her alone. By the end of the drive exhaustion had set in, but he'd ridden Emmet to the Halverson camp to learn Libby had just driven off with her grandmother. "My mom's in need of a hot bath and a long nap." Imogene explained. "I'm impressed a woman in her eighties was able to keep up."

"Yes, ma'am." Evan's disappointment must have been evident.

Imogene placed a hand on Emmet's neck and looked up.

Libby had Imogene's full mouth and high cheek bones. He hated himself for it, but he felt like a small boy again. Only it wasn't his mother's displeasure he'd caused—it was Libby's, too.

He'd been an impulsive idiot to dance with Angela.

Imogene's voice was kind. "It was an inconsiderate thing to do. You need to apologize. But if you love her, you'll figure out a way to prove it." Imogene's expression was motherly. "Yes, I read your mind. Or rather, your face." She chuckled and patted his hand. "Evan, you might not realize this, but when you danced your first dance since...well, your first dance in all these years, with a woman Libby considered a rival for your affection when she was a teenager, you reopened the wounds her daddy left behind. To Libby, you chose someone besides her to share something really important with."

Evan's stomach dropped another level every time Imogene elaborated to make her point.

After Imogene left, Cody came to help him down from his saddle. "You look stiff. I sure am. Give me your reins, and I'll take your horse." He sniffed in Evan's direction and wrinkled his nose. "No wonder Libby wouldn't go near you. You smell like roadkill."

"Very funny." Evan handed Cody his reins. "You don't smell any better than I do."

"Molly will kiss me anyway. Wanna make a bet? Or maybe you've sworn off wagering on women?" Cody raised a mocking brow.

Evan glowered and gave Cody a shove. "Sometimes you take things too far."

Cody dipped his head, a smile playing around his mouth. "Sorry. Couldn't resist. You sure made a muddle of things, brother."

With anvils instead of feet—or rather, foot and prosthetic —Evan was suddenly too tired to argue or even walk. "Gimme my horse back."

Cody shook his head. "No. Go shower and have a swim. I'll sort your horse."

An hour later Evan was slumped in a lounge chair, not having made it all the way into the pool. A magpie cocked its head and blinked black marble eyes at him from its perch on a lime tree limb. It flew away when Mrs. M set a tray of lemonade on the table. "Thanks," Evan said.

Mrs. M answered with a heavy sigh and shake of her head.

"Not you, too?"

"You had to go and dance with Angela Macey of all people?" She poured him a glass. Without garnishes.

"I'll take some, too." Grandpa Smokey groaned as he lowered himself in the next chair over.

Evan glanced at him. Grandpa looked shriveled today. A bit like a raisin with gray hair and stubble covering the lower half of his face and neck.

Grandpa Smokey took the lemonade—with sugared lemon wedge and mint—from Mrs. M with a nod of thanks. "I do believe I just took the longest shower of my life, yet I'm still sore."

Evan grunted.

He could sense Grandpa Smokey's eyes on him. "Try the hot tub."

Sipping his lemonade, Grandpa kept one shrewd eye on Evan. "How long do you plan on sittin' around feelin' sorry for yourself?"

Evan tossed a pebble at the magpie who had returned to eavesdrop.

"Well?"

"I don't know what to do," Evan said. He was miserable. Libby had always been hard to reach but now that he'd hurt her, he might never scale her walls again.

"Me neither, but you got to do somethin' after making that girl feel like a fool in front of the whole camp. Not to mention breaking her heart after all she's done for you."

"Do you have to rub my nose in this?" Evan dragged a hand through his hair. The magpie landed again, cocked his head.

"He's mocking you," Grandpa said in a dry tone. "You know birds mate for life?"

Evan gave him a narrow look and pushed himself up. He didn't have to listen to this unhelpful—

"Sit back. I know you're hurting too."

Evan sighed. He was too weary to leave anyway.

"You must fight for love sometimes. The Bible says it's harder to scale the walls of a city than someone you've offended."

Evan knew he'd heard that phrase somewhere.

"But it doesn't say it's impossible, just difficult. You're familiar with difficult." Grandpa Smokey grunted and crossed his feet at the ankles.

"I can't believe I was so stupid."

"Me neither. But it was just a mistake and a chance for Libby to get used to forgivin' you." Grandpa chuckled. "That bird there is the perfect example of what you need."

Evan eyed the magpie, preening its feathers with one beady, black eye on them. "What's that?"

"Perseverance in the face of adversity. Here you are throwing rocks, and he just comes back." Grandpa groaned and creaked as he stood, retrieved his half-empty lemonade, and shuffled inside the house.

Evan sat holding his breath, having a stare down with the bird. Moments seemed to crawl by before he finally released the breath and blinked. "Jerk."

"Arguing with a bird, huh?" Seth laughed and sat in the seat Grandpa Smokey had vacated. Couldn't anyone leave him alone?

"Something like that."

"Sounds like I missed plenty of drama…wild dogs, Angela…" Seth held up fingers. "And I heard Dawson bragging about dancing with Libby."

"Too bad you missed it all."

"Heard your grandfather give Dawson an earful, too. I think he's sending him off somewhere for a while."

"Really?" Evan sat straighter. At least he wasn't the only guy on the sharp end of Grandpa Smokey's temper.

Seth gulped down Evan's lemonade and poured another glass. "Sounds like the cattle drive was more interesting than flying a plane over the mountains in high winds."

"Glad you came home in one piece. You think a guy would learn his lesson after crashing a plane once before. You and Cody were lucky to be found alive." He tossed another pebble at the magpie. The bird squawked and flew up, landing on the fence again and impaling Evan with a glare.

"That bird's a worthy opponent, he's not giving up."

Evan stretched to reach a rock the size of a hen's egg.

Seth clamped a hand on his wrist. "Put it down, that little bird isn't your Goliath." He knocked the rock out of Evan's hand. "I have an idea that might win you some Libby points." Reaching inside his pocket, he pulled out a neat stack of bills, and placed it on the table.

"What's that?"

"The wager money Dawson went around collecting at the cattle drive. Clint Jeffers picked it up and told me to give it to you. Said you earned it fair and square, but you left it in the dirt."

"Let me guess. Out of the kindness of his dried up, blackened heart?"

Seth laughed. "Something like that." He pinched a lemon slice from the tray and popped it into his mouth, chewed without a grimace, and chose another. "I'm not going to say what you already know, but man, you need to make it up to Libby. Sooner rather than later if you don't want your heart to get stomped on a regular basis."

"My dad told me they hired Libby as a therapist for all the McClure ranches." He was both relieved Libby had reason to stay and simultaneously eaten up that he'd run off another woman he loved. Seeing her often but having her hate him was going to be a kick in the gut every time.

"Don't mean she won't leave. She could change her mind now that she's got hurt feelings about that dance."

A dagger lanced Evan's heart. Grandpa Smokey was right, he shouldn't just shut down again, indulge his tendency toward self-pity. He hadn't wronged his mother, and he'd done nothing wrong to Angela. But Libby was another matter. He'd have to make it right because he wanted her back. Wanted the wedding, the kids, and everything else that meant. Heck, he'd even build Libby a custom home and her own clinic, give her every reason to stay in Apple Valley.

They'd focused on him and his recovery long enough.

Seth leaned forward with his hands between his knees. "Sorry, bro. I meant that Libby doesn't seem the type to stay in one place. You should act fast. Want to hear my idea to score some points with that little firecracker you're so crazy about?"

Seth wasn't known for his skill in the romance department. In fact, quite the opposite. His on and off again relationship with Charmaine was exhibit A. But he was a good friend for trying to boost morale. Evan lifted a shoulder. "Okay, shoot."

"So, this is what we do…"

Evan leaned in to catch Seth's lowered voice. God love him, the guy sure had a lot of try in him.

~

"ARE you sure he's not going to toss us out?" Evan turned to Seth, standing on Lefty's porch with a handful of photos.

"No, but it's worth a try, don't you think?"

Evan snatched the photos and climbed the last stair. He strode to the door of Lefty's—no, Libby's—house, and knocked with a knuckle.

The door cracked open. When Lefty's shifty eyes landed on Seth, he opened it the rest of the way with a smile. "Seth, glad you made it out."

"Uncle." Seth nodded. "You remember Evan McClure, Alex's son?"

"Veteran and former football QB. How could I forget? I rode a float in the parade to welcome you home from war. Come on inside boys."

Evan was pretty sure by 'rode a float' Lefty meant passed out drunk on a truck bed.

Seated around the table with a fresh pot of coffee and a plate of muffins, Evan marveled at the cleanliness of the place. Seth's plan might just have merit.

"And here's a photo of the one I told you about yesterday. The guy who lost his arm. See how his kid is behind him on Theo's old pony? Yeah. He's smiling."

"So, all those guys are combat-wounded vets?" Lefty scratched his stubbly jaw. Evan noted two missing fingers.

"They had a great week with their families, but one week

out of a year…well, we all know it isn't enough. And it was only a handful of guys. We could do so much more."

Lefty bobbed his head. A light twinkled in the old man's eyes. Evan hadn't seen him for at least a dozen years before today. Lefty used to be the town drunk. Some years back Grandpa Smokey and Hamish Cameron, Libby's grandfather, had sent him somewhere to dry up and then housed him here. That's all Evan knew.

"What more can you do?" Lefty leaned forward with his elbows on the table.

"Evan here would like to have retreats once a month from early summer to late fall. Maybe even expand past that, depending on the number of volunteers we're able to raise." Evan nodded, content to let Seth do the talking until he remembered a detail that might help their cause. "I understand you were in Vietnam, like my grandfather."

A cloud crossed Lefty's face. "Bad times."

"You can sympathize with other veterans. As a combat-wounded vet myself, that's how I'm choosing to see things." Evan's throat started to tighten.

"Me, too." Seth offered. He took a sip of his coffee. He was giving Lefty time to absorb their words. Evan knew his friend well. Seth was cunning, but also kind. The solution he'd come up with would benefit everyone, including Lefty.

"You can help other vets, including the friends who helped you here in Apple Valley," Seth said.

"You mean Smokey and Hamish."

Seth shrugged. "And their wives and children."

Several emotions played over Lefty's face as his eyes darted around the kitchen. He was fond of this place, that was plain enough.

Evan pulled out the rolled up plans he'd brought along in a cardboard tube and laid them out on the table, using their coffee cups to pin down the corners. "This would be your new home, here." Evan pointed to the architect's rough plan. A cabin, next to the bunkhouse, with the addition of three more, stood next to a new barn, round pen, and off to one side, a small chapel. "See, you'd have privacy, and the cabin would be deeded to you for the remainder of your life by contract." He'd solve their problems by offering Lefty a home on the Three M and a purpose for his days.

Seth traded a glance with Evan, then turned to his uncle. "And you'd oversee the staff and volunteers who run the program. You'd be the hospitality coordinator, or whatever you want to call it."

Lefty's bushy eyebrows pinched together. "Why can't I do that from my own house?" He tapped a stubbed finger on the table.

"Uncle," Seth used a soothing voice. "Be reasonable. Those people are going to need a lot of care. The staff will need guidance around the clock. Your sacrifice and service to your fellow veterans and their families might even save some-one's life. You know the suicide rates, and you can't even imagine the divorce rates. PTSD damages their minds as much as bullets and bombs chew up their outsides."

Lefty's face clouded again. He traced the outline of the

little cabin on the plans. "I'd live there year round? What would I do when there ain't no retreats goin' on?"

"You'd oversee things like weekly cleaning, repairs, you know…all the things any foreman might do. Besides, you'll see to the maintenance of the outside of the cabins, too. We'll want landscaping. There will be the care of a string of ponies and riding horses. Besides that, we hope to put in a pool in the next couple of years."

"Won't the wranglers see to them horses?" Lefty squinted at Evan.

"No. They don't have time. It's a big responsibility, I admit. So, if you don't think you can do this…" He pasted on a doubtful expression.

Lefty straightened in his chair.

Seth shot Evan an amused look. "Maybe he's a bit too old for the job?"

Evan pretended concern. It had the desired effect.

"I can handle it with one hand tied behind my back," Lefty pounded the table in outrage.

"I believe you." Evan held out his hand and Lefty shook on the deal.

"We'll break ground on your cabin first, Uncle. Should have a crew on the job right away."

They stayed and shot the breeze for another quarter of an hour before Seth signaled it was time to go.

"Told you it would work." Outside, Seth's smile was smug.

"How'd you know?" Evan would have bet good money Lefty would refuse. He was dug in there at Libby's place and even sewed himself curtains and cushions. Evan had never seen the like of such a cozy house inhabited by a crusty, disreputable bachelor. Libby's house wasn't trashed, like he'd assumed it would be.

"Lefty needs to feel valuable. He put all his care into that house and his dog."

"I didn't see any dog."

"My point. His old dog died, and I know Lefty's been lonely. You see all those plants he tends inside and out?"

"Now that you mention it."

"He likes to take care of things. I just took a gamble that given the opportunity, he'd transfer his care over to people. People he could relate with. Who better than veterans with problems?"

"You're smarter than I give you credit for." Evan tightened his seatbelt. Seth drove his truck like his plane. Never mind obstacles in the road.

Seth rolled his eyes. "Too bad I can't say the same."

"Sometimes I'd like to punch you in the nose." Evan glared at the road ahead.

Chapter 18

STOMPING THE TWO-STEP

One leg swinging over the other, Grandma Rose fiddled with her big silver hoop earrings . Her eyes pinned Libby to the sofa in the living room. "Love stays and fights, Libby. It doesn't act scared and run off when there's a problem."

"Maybe it isn't love then." Libby stroked Pumpkin's head. She was being obstinate, but Gram brought that out in her. The dog rested her chin on Libby's knee. A tall glass of iced tea dripped condensation on Mom's antique cherry wood table.

"You've loved that boy for as long as either of us can remember. Stop being pig-headed. So he danced with another woman? So what?" Gram threw her hands up.

"Another woman? It wasn't just any woman, or I wouldn't care. It was his former fiancé, and it wasn't just any dance. It was The Dance. The two-step he bet me he would dance when we discussed his goals. That was supposed to be our dance.

Not his and Angela's." Libby's chest heaved and nostrils flared. The memory of Evan and Angela clasping hands while everyone circled around them was seared into the inside of her eyelids.

Pumpkin's ears lifted, and she stared at Libby.

Grandma Rose sniffed. "It was unfortunate. I don't blame you for being upset, just as long as you're not jealous. Jealousy is petty. Besides, everyone knows Evan's heart belongs to nobody but you."

"How could he do it? How could he share something so... so symbolic with Angela? I gave him everything I had."

"No." Gram looked her in the eye. "You didn't. You've held your heart back ever since your daddy left. Don't you think it's time you healed from that? You're not a child anymore."

"I'm not sure if you realize how cold you sound sometimes." Libby sent a cutting glare in Gram's direction.

"Cold? Not at all. Do you think it would be kinder to let you stew in your own juices forever? Would it be kind to allow Evan to sit in a wheelchair until the end of his days? No. Kindness is not turning away when someone you love needs help to grow."

"This is different."

"It most certainly is not. People can be maimed inside as well as out. But—" She jabbed the air with her finger. "We have the power to choose love and reject fear. Fear is the absence of love. God wired us for love because He is love." She patted Libby's knee. "Love produces trust, faith, kindness, patience, and security. Things like that bathe our brains in chemicals that produce feelings of well-being. They allow us to live above our feelings and circumstances to make choices that reflect the heart of God."

Libby blinked at Gram. "Um…that was a lot of words."

"You're smart. Don't act dumb."

"Where do you learn this stuff?"

"It's brain science—neuroplasticity—the ability to rewire our own brains. You should try it." Grandma Rose lifted her chin.

Libby was thinking up a retort when the front door opened. Mom came inside loaded with a bag of groceries. Theo and Bella tussled behind her. Gram's dogs, Bonnie and Clyde jumped from their bed and began the ruckus they always did when the kids came to visit and brought their dogs. Pumpkin released a deep, happy-sounding woof.

Gram stood with a creaking of her knees. "Think about what I said, child." She held her arms open for Theo. "Hello, darlings. Come for dinner, have you?"

"We're sleeping over. I get to make the salad tonight." Bella took the bag of groceries from Mom and skipped into the kitchen.

Theo collapsed with the four small dogs. When they all settled down into a pile he hopped up and sat beside Libby on the sofa. "Aunt Libby, we was at the Books & Brew when we heard a gossip."

Libby mustered a half smile for Theo, but she was still stirring around the things Gram had said to her. "Listening to gossip never works out, buddy."

Theo shook his head. "Nope. Mrs. Pearson was sayin' that Uncle Evan is a turd. But he ain't!"

Libby's head snapped up. "Who was she talking to?"

"Another lady I didn't know. Bella don't know either, I already asked." Theo's expression was troubled. Evan was his hero.

"I'm sorry you heard nasty comments about your uncle. You know it isn't true. Evan is a good guy."

Theo fingered Clyde's ear. The old corgi leaned against Theo's leg in bliss. "Mrs. Pearson said Uncle Evan done you wrong, and she wouldn't blame you if you never talked to him ever again."

Libby sat back against the sofa and sighed. Theo mimicked her and tucked himself under her arm, snuggling beside her. He loved with a pure heart, and she envied him that. He didn't hide his emotions. When he needed comfort, he got it. When he was upset, he said so. When he was happy, he let it show. "We could all learn a thing or two from you, buddy." Libby kissed Theo's head and pulled him in tighter.

"Are you gonna leave and never come back?" There was a quiver in his voice that punched Libby's heart. "One of the cowboys said that's what you'd do, and I think Uncle Evan is sad about it." Theo lifted his little hand to her jaw and turned her to look into his eyes. "I think he was crying 'cause his eyes was red and his mouth was facing down."

All her years of keeping her distance suddenly felt very selfish.

"Theo, I love you, and I love my whole family. I'm sorry I stayed away before, but I'm back now, and I'm not leaving again. I don't want to miss you and the girls growing up."

She'd missed too much already. The truth was, leaving everything she loved was just chicken-hearted. Including Evan. Molly was right. She had coped with her problems just like their father. The very person she'd blamed all these years.

Theo tugged Libby off the couch. "Turn on some music, Aunt Libby. Mrs. Pearson said Uncle Evan broke your heart 'cause you wanted to dance. I can dance with you, then your heart will be happy."

Libby laughed, thumbed open her phone screen to her music app, and chose an upbeat song.

"Uncle Evan ain't married because ladies like to dance. Maybe I can teach him so he can get married now." Theo wore a calculating look.

Stifling a snort, Libby pointed to her feet. "Maybe you'd better learn the steps before you try to teach them to your uncle."

"I gotta learn so I can dance with Mandy Jenkins at the Cattlemen's Ball. Mama got me a new shirt, and I'm gonna get my hair cut, too."

She'd promised to go to that ball as Evan's date if he danced the two-step by his Alive Day. He had, even if it wasn't with her. Gram's words rang in her ears. We can choose love and reject fear.

But hadn't she chosen fear most of the time? Wasn't that why she found a reason to push away every guy who'd shown any kind of interest in her since she was old enough to date? Wasn't fear, or the byproducts of it, the reason she'd avoided spending much time in her hometown where Evan was rooted?

Evan wasn't going anywhere. Apple Valley's graveyard held generations of McClure bones. Maybe deep down, knowing Evan wasn't likely to ever leave this town was one of the reasons her heart was drawn to him. But she'd always known her feelings for Evan went beyond infatuation. In her honest moments, she'd admitted she was in love, and that had scared her. Loving someone meant they had the power to wreck you. Or the power to help you heal.

Libby prayed silent, pleading prayers while she counted the steps out for Theo.

"THAT WILL BE three hundred and twenty-four dollars, Mr. McClure." The elderly cashier's eyes were magnified behind her thick, gold-framed glasses.

Evan handed her the wager money, stacked in neat bills. "Keep the change. Did you double-check the delivery address?"

"Yes, twice." She ran his card. "I hope she's worth it. That's quite a lot of money." She shot him a narrow look.

"She is." He slipped his card back into his wallet and steered through the sweet-smelling roses, carnations, and other flowers he couldn't name. "Thank you." He closed the door behind him and took a breath of fresh air. The cloying scents inside the floristry shop made him want to sneeze.

He checked his watch as he crossed the dirt road and climbed into his truck. He didn't want to be late for his meeting with Troy McBride. The carpenter came highly recommended and was hard to contract. He'd need to squeeze a tux fitting into an already tight schedule today, too. Funny to think that this time last year he rarely left the house and almost never left the ranch.

Libby had come along and changed everything. He'd never consider attending the Cattlemen's Ball if it wasn't for how she'd built up his ego and pushed him to keep going no matter how rough things got. And they'd gotten plenty rough. She had a way of making him feel like he was that goofy kid again who'd conned himself into thinking he was invincible.

Now he knew for sure that life was going to knock him on his butt again. But he'd get back up because God was on his side. Because God loved him when he was the captain of the football team, when he was dug into the sand dodging bullets and bombs, and even when he was the guy with two weeks' worth of stubble on his cheeks wheeling himself around the house in a fog of self-pity.

He couldn't earn God's love and the revelation brought nothing but relief. He was fair tired of trying to earn his way by being top dog at everything.

Bella had planted the seeds of acceptance a couple of years

ago. But Libby had watered them and plucked out a few weeds, to stick with the gardening metaphors.

Hopefully, Libby liked the flowers he'd just bought for her. Hopefully, they said what he hadn't found the courage to say, and hopefully, she felt the same way. Hopefully, she'd give him the opportunity to apologize for what he was realizing was a real jerk move. Dancing with Angela had seemed harmless at the time.

When Seth described the pain on Libby's face that night, he hadn't spared Evan's feelings. "Dude, you crushed her. I can't believe you gave away your victory dance to Angela. What's up with you?" Seth had given him a scathing look and stalked off.

Being more like brothers than friends, they were back to bad jokes and backslaps by the next day, but it took a lot for Seth to criticize him. He didn't do it often, so when he did Evan took his words to heart.

When he was with Libby, he was a whole man again. She believed in him. More to the point, he believed in her. She was a strong woman who loved the same things he did.

And he'd stomped the two-step over Libby's heart.

He pulled to the side of the road and parked his truck. He had a lot to accomplish today if his plans were going to come together.

Chapter 19

EMERALDS & PRODIGALS

"The dress you bought for the Cattlemen's Ball is gorgeous." Libby smiled as Molly danced around Libby's bedroom, peering into the full-length mirror at her reflection.

"Isn't it? I plan to keep Cody's eyes right here." Molly turned to get a rear view of the pale blue, backless gown. An exact match for her eyes. She turned to Libby with pinched brows. "I wish Josie would fly in for the ball."

"Me too, but she would just outshine us all. You're going to burn Cody's retinas in that dress."

"That's the plan."

The afternoon sun cast short shadows on the floor, and the September sky from her window was almost as stunning as her beautiful sister.

Molly dimpled. "Tell me you are going to wear that dazzling green number?"

"I bought that when I thought I was going to the ball with Evan."

"You didn't exactly give him a chance to explain himself."

Libby knotted her arms over her chest.

"Evan isn't the kind of man to pursue a woman he thinks hates him."

"I don't hate him." Is that what Evan thought?

"Mrs. Landis, who owns the florist's place, said Evan ordered over three hundred dollars' worth of flowers. I can only assume they were for you. What did you do with them?" Molly made slits of her eyes.

Libby hadn't considered the cost of so many roses. "Maybe I discouraged Evan more than I meant to."

"You threw them away?"

Libby shook her head.

"Tossed them at his head?"

Libby nearly cracked a smile. "No. I just...ignored them."

"The way you felt he ignored your feelings." Molly examined her.

"I guess Dolly the Llama ate them. The delivery person left them on the porch the day she got loose."

"So, if you're not going to forgive Evan—and I'm not offering an opinion on that—have you thought what your life will be like without him?" Molly tilted her head to one side. "Have you thought this through?"

"I'll keep busy with my work." Libby shrugged as if life without Evan would be no big deal, but her stomach turned over. Evan was the standard she'd measured all other men against. Nobody else had come close.

"Your face tells another story," Molly said with a knowing look. "I love you, so I'm pretty ticked at Evan, but you have never been in love with any other guy, big sister. Besides, forgiveness sets you free. I'm an expert on that."

Libby swiped a hand over eyes.

"You're smearing your mascara. Grandma Rose would tell you to freshen up and go get your man. I used to think her advice was ridiculous, but the older I get the more I admire her boldness."

"I should have just given Evan an earful that night." Libby blew out a painful breath. "But I played the memory of it over and over until it seemed even worse than it probably was." Libby worried her bottom lip and met Molly's eyes. "I can't stand the thought of being so vulnerable."

Molly slipped off her dress and hung it in the garment bag. She squirmed into her sundress. "That sounds like a bad case of pride to me. Sorry, but I can judge that book because I wrote it. My pride cost Cody and me a lot of happiness. Not to mention the years it stole from Bella and Theo." She straightened her hair. "Thanks for letting me keep my dress here. I don't want Cody to get nosy and find it before the ball."

"No problem." Libby sat in the window seat and picked at the stitches in a pillow.

Molly pressed a wrinkle out of her dress. "I think Evan is really sorry for dancing with his ex. I suspect he wants to make it up to you."

Libby chewed her nail and watched the sun sink lower.

"Did you hear me?" Molly asked.

"I heard you. Why do you think that?"

"He's up to something. He's had Lefty at the ranch a couple of times."

Libby scooted her back against the window frame and swung her legs up onto the seat. "Lefty went to the Three M?"

Molly shrugged. "I know, weird. Seth wasn't even around."

"Maybe he's just being nice to Lefty. Evan is just like that. I told him how lonely Lefty seems."

"How are you going to deal with your feelings for Evan? Because ignoring them isn't healthy."

"Eat a pan of brownies?"

Molly chuckled and rolled her eyes. She sat next to Libby and pulled her into a hug. "Guys can be so dense about romance sometimes. If it helps, Cody says Evan's crazy about you."

"He wanted to explain. I didn't give him the chance."

"I've lived in the same house with him for two years now, and I've come to love him like a brother. I can honestly say he's not the kind of guy to purposely hurt you."

"I didn't think so either—until the cattle drive."

Molly kissed Libby's cheek. "Gotta go, Rose will be waking from her nap." She hesitated at the door, then turned to face Libby. "Wear the emerald dress to the Cattlemen's Ball." Her mouth turned down. "Evan isn't Dad. You can trust him, Lib. He's kind. He's loyal." She lowered her eyes. "Well, there was the dance thing, but that's the only time I've seen him act like a pudding head."

Libby chuckled. "Pudding head?"

"I guess I'm used to having conversations in front of children." Molly grinned and closed the bedroom door behind her.

Gazing at the dress she'd bought with Evan in mind, Libby ran through possible scenarios. Should she even go to the ball? She hadn't attended in years. It was going to be awkward. During the past several months she'd taken on Evan's successes and failures as her own without sharing much of herself.

Her heart was battered at the memory of Angela and Evan's hands twined in victory. She'd felt robbed of what she and Evan had done together. But she had to admit, she'd purposely kept him an arm's length away.

The door creaked open, and Grandma Rose slipped inside, shutting it behind her. She sat on the patchwork quilt covering Libby's bed. They'd made it together from Grandpa Cameron's flannel shirts after he'd died. Libby had refused to wash them before cutting the squares, and one or two still smelled faintly of Grandpa's cologne. Mom claimed that was just her imagination, but Gram took her side. She had a matching quilt on her bed downstairs.

"I brought you my emerald chandelier earrings for the ball." Gram dangled a pair of gorgeous earrings.

"Those were a gift from Grandpa. I can't wear them. Besides, I haven't even decided if I'm going."

"Oh, you're going." Grandma Rose sometimes took a tone.

Smart people heeded the warning. "These earrings were indeed a gift from your granddad. When he gave them to me, he said he doubted I needed more courage, but these were the kind that would supply extra." She pursed her lips. "If he were here, he'd tell me to offer them to you. Libby, my dear, you're at a place in your life where you need to decide something important."

Libby stood up and paced in front of the window seat. "Actually, Gram, I have several things I need to decide."

"Chief among them being, my girl, whether or not you're going to let love slip out of your grasp."

Libby paused in front of the window. "Love is a slippery thing, isn't it?"

"It can be." The apples of Gram's cheeks bunched in a smile. "So often in the eye of an emotional storm, we don't use our capacity to step outside of our feelings. It's hard to be objective in those moments."

"Is there anything objective about love?"

"It takes skill to live above your feelings." She wagged a finger in Libby's direction. "The whims of hormones, blood sugars, or bad moods aren't to be trusted. They cause us to say and do stupid things occasionally."

Libby collapsed on the bed beside Grandma Rose and melted into her waiting arms.

"You need to embrace your blessings as well as your trials."

"No more lectures, please."

Gram twitched her nose. "It's my job." She held out her

hand with the earrings sparkling in her palm. "Take a risk for once in your life. Go to the ball, Cinderella, and dance with your rancher prince."

They giggled while Libby tried the earrings on. She crossed the room to look in the mirror and liked the way they swayed and tinkled. "These are the moment, aren't they? I don't dare to even wear a necklace with them."

Grandma Rose nodded in approval. "They are the moment, indeed."

The emeralds glinted from her lobes.

She reached behind her and clasped Gram's hand. "Thank you."

CODY STRAIGHTENED his silver bolo tie and adjusted the turquoise piece in the full-length mirror on the closet door. "Molly was looking for you. Said you need to talk before we leave for the ball," Evan said.

He and Cody were dressing in Nate's old room where they'd taken to storing things like suits and dress boots. The youngest McClure brother hadn't been inside his bedroom for years. Mrs. M kept it like a museum after he packed a duffel and said he and his band were going on a summer tour.

"What did I do? Is Molly mad?" Cody's forehead creased with the kind of panicked look only a married man wore.

Evan shrugged in a how-should-I-know manner and adjusted the shoulder seam on his suit jacket, then yanked down the pant leg that covered his prosthetic. It wasn't hanging quite right, and he wanted everything perfect tonight.

Cody fumbled with clumsy, weather-swollen fingers not meant for pearl buttons. "Make a big deal out of the bolo ties Molly made. She wants us to look sharp on the stage when they recognize Dad and Grandpa Smokey." He rubbed at the silver-tipped toe of his boot. Molly had gotten her hands on those, too.

Evan had taken precautions and hidden his.

Slapping cologne on his neck, Cody eyed Evan in mirror. "Nate's a real jerk for not answering our calls. Too big for his britches, I guess. Dad won't say it, but I know he's pining to have Nate with us tonight."

"The least we can do is try to make Dad proud." A vinegar taste burned its way up Evan's throat. Between his little brother and their mother, Dad's heart had really taken a beating over the years.

A honeyed, yet somehow still bossy voice came from the doorway. "I'm going to need you guys to collect the shirt sizes of all the wranglers on the Three M. I've designed new T-shirt swag, so you guys better get used to matching." Molly leaned against the doorjamb with her hands in her robe pockets and grinned. Her pale hair was piled on her head, and she'd put on make-up.

Evan and Cody locked horrified eyes. Evan pinched the bridge of his nose, eyed Molly warily and said, "You know this ranch seemed barren when we only had poor Mrs. M here, but it might be easier on us men if you took over at a slower pace. I'm not sure we can induce those cowboys to go from showering once a month to wearing matching clothes."

Cody shook with silent laughter next to him.

"Well, the girls are here now, so get used to it." Molly's nostrils flared. "Come here, Evan. Let me help you get this bolo to hang properly."

"Give it up. You can't win," Cody whispered.

Evan shrugged and stepped forward obediently. It was good to see Cody so happy. He'd struggled as a single father. Marriage looked good on him. And Evan was certain he'd find Theo spit-shined and wearing a matching bolo and boots to Cody's.

Cody fixed soft eyes on his dainty wife as she stood on tiptoes to adjust the bolo around Evan's neck. His brother was smitten, and it was painful to watch.

"You look like a cowboy rockstar." Molly smiled and patted Evan's shoulder.

"Thanks, but I'll save that title for Nate," Evan quipped. "Too bad he's missing another Cattlemen's Ball. He loved to dance with all the moms when he was a kid. A real charmer, that one."

Molly turned to give her husband a quick kiss. "I'm going to get dressed. Let's meet downstairs in thirty minutes." She dropped Cody a flirty look. "I might call you if I need help."

"Sure, sweetheart." Cody's eyes darted to Evan after she disappeared down the hall.

Evan smirked, but his gut pinched with a hint of envy at

the happy couple. He shook it off. "Nate would be the first to ask Mrs. M to dance."

"You bet he would," Cody agreed. "I'm partnering with my wife for the opening dance, but I'll take Mrs. M around the floor next."

"That's if I don't get to her first," Evan said with a challenging flash of teeth.

"Neither one of you is faster than me," said a deep voice from the hall.

Cody and Evan both looked toward the doorway. They froze when a beefy figure in military fatigues crossed the threshold.

"What are you guys doing in my room?" Nate McClure, sporting a crew cut, crossed his muscular arms over a very broad chest and stared them down from a height of at least six-foot-four.

The beast in the doorway was scrawny Nate?

They erupted in shouts, whoops of laughter, and a few manly tears might have leaked from Evan's eyes.

Cody wrapped Nate's knees in a hug, lifted him, and lugged him across the room. He tossed him on the bed and toppled over a pair of boots on the floor.

"Dude, you're going to rip your pretty clothes, and I think your wife will have something to say about that." Nate cracked a smile, folded his hands behind his head, and gazed at Cody and Evan with a look that said he'd gotten one over on them.

"Why didn't you tell us you were coming home?" Cody stood over Nate's prostrated form. "Tonight's the—"

"I know what tonight is. I have a suit with me." Nate's features changed from playful boy to soulful man. "I couldn't let Dad down again. Or you guys."

Nate was different, and it wasn't just the uniform. The last time they'd laid eyes on him, he was too skinny and had greasy hair down the middle of his back.

"I joined up a few years ago but didn't tell you guys because…I knew how you'd feel about it after what happened to Evan." Special Forces with experience was written into the premature lines around Nate's mouth and eyes. He wasn't a bad-tempered puppy anymore. Nate was a dangerous warrior.

Evan cocked his head. "Where's that suit you told us you brought along?" He swallowed the fear in the pit of his gut. His little brother was in the military?

"In my truck. I'll put it on after I see Dad and Smokey."

"Does Dad know you're here?" Cody studied Nate with narrowed eyes.

Nate shook his head. "He's about to find out." He stood, impressive and wholly unfamiliar. Cat-like nonchalance and confidence radiated off him as if bullets would bounce off his chest in a shootout.

But Evan knew better. He'd been like that once, too, and found out bullets—or rockets—did indeed damage a man who'd thought himself invincible. He prayed silently that God would protect his brother and bring him home for good someday—in one piece.

Chapter 20

THE CATTLEMEN'S BALL

The event center had been transformed. Twinkle lights, silver and gold balloons, and rich blue satin covered tables. Tripods in corner groupings featured photos of famous bulls, stud horses, or cattlemen.

"Very patriotic," Mom observed.

Libby's eyes flitted from face to face. "There must be close to three hundred people here."

"More." Mom pulled her toward a group of tables at the far end of the room, but Libby dragged her feet, ears chasing the sound of music to a full band on the stage. They wore black tie with cowboy hats. Every table featured champagne glasses, fine porcelain, and centerpieces of white roses with sprays of bright green ferns. Simple and elegant.

They skirted the dance floor and dodged servers carrying trays of frosty-looking cider and beer, wine, and champagne bottles. Everything on the menu was locally sourced. It was a matter of pride to their agricultural community.

"Molly saved us seats at Alex's table." Mom dipped her head in acknowledgment to Ross McClure at the next table. Her smile was breezy, but a rosy flush climbed her throat.

Libby hid an amused smile. She tried to be polite to those at the table but couldn't help sneaking furtive glances around, hoping to see Evan.

Molly leaned into the table. "You know you're somebody when the Cattleman's Association sets aside an entire section of the room for you and your family." She tipped her head to indicate Smokey, distinguished in a western suit, boots, and a white Stetson. "He's all smiles. Nate McClure came home for the ball."

"They must be relieved." Libby searched but didn't see anyone who looked like a rockstar near the McClure tables.

Three women gliding past them like a queen and her consorts stopped to chat with Molly.

"Who are they?" Libby asked after their brief stop.

Molly tipped her head near Libby's ear. She looked like a Christmas vision in the icy blue gown. "The Bradley women. You mean to say you've never heard of them?" Molly's eyes went wide when Libby shook her head. "They own Bradley Boots. Sylvia Bradley inherited sole ownership after her husband died. Haley and Cicely, her daughters, are targets for fortune hunters." Molly pointed. "See their lariat necklaces?"

Libby obliged by peeking at the trio. "Gorgeous. I mean, not as nice as anything you might make…"

"I did make those." Molly laughed. Her eyes were sparkling with happiness. "They ordered matching pieces months ago. Look over there." She directed Libby's attention to a man with a camera. "Magazine coverage. I'm going to hire help. Molly McClure Designs will be backordered for a year after tonight. The Bradley women set western fashion standards." She gave Libby a conspiratorial look, complete with arched brow.

Libby was about to reply when Evan appeared in her line of vision. The Bradley sisters were eyeing him like he was a juicy steak. He looked like rancher royalty. His black tuxedo, worn with a bolo, cowboy boots, and a gray Stetson made sparks dance down her spine.

But it was the emerald green silk pocket square that made her heart go wild.

THE CROWDED EVENT center teased Evan's nerves. The last thing he wanted to do was get knocked sideways, fall, and make a fool of himself. The room was stifling, and the murmur of hundreds of voices, like droning bees, distracted him from his mission—to find Libby.

Nate danced past him with Mrs. M in his huge arms. The look on her face was worth millions. He clapped his little brother on the back and continued to wade through cowboys, ranchers, farmers, businessmen, and beautiful women in eye-dazzling dresses, draped in everything from diamonds to turquoise.

But Evan was searching for emeralds.

Finally, he glimpsed Libby at the Three M table. His heart thumped with pleasure at the sight. She was so beautiful. He loved her and he was going to tell her so. As soon as he had enough spit in his mouth to do it.

After years of fighting his limits and failing, he was finally coming to terms with his new body. Thanks to Libby, it was getting easier to accept that his identity had never been defined by his somewhat limited abilities. Libby had helped him without even realizing that her contribution was not just therapy for his body, but for his soul. He couldn't do without her.

The ranch foreman, Bertie Valdez stepped beside him and bumped shoulders. "What are you waiting for man? Go get her."

Heart racing, Evan squared his shoulders and headed toward his future.

THE LOOK of admiration and desire in Evan's eyes as he stood in front of her and stared turned Libby's legs into noodles. She wanted to run into his arms, but her feet had grown roots.

She needn't have worried because after a buttery smile split Evan's handsome face, he came to her, barely limping at all, and her heart swelled at that.

Evan tilted his head and held out his hands. Libby tangled her fingers in his and looked at him through her lashes. Good thing she'd applied waterproof mascara.

"I'm sorry. Libby, I'm so very sorry for dancing our two-step with Angela. It was hurtful and ungrateful and...my ego—"

Libby wrangled a hand loose and pressed a finger to Evan's lips. "I forgive you. I shouldn't have quit you like I did. I should have been more truthful and let you know how I felt sooner." She squeezed his hands then brought them to her mouth and kissed his work-roughened knuckles.

Evan's eyes crinkled at the corners when he locked his dreamy blues on her. He pulled her into his arms and kissed her until her knees gave out and he had to steady her. Everyone near enough to witness them stopped to clap and whistle.

Breathless, Libby dragged her lips from his.

Evan peered around them and chuckled. The sound rumbled from his chest where Libby had glued herself. She shivered when he pressed his mouth to her ear. "I love you, Elizabeth Halverson. I should have told you sooner."

Holding Evan's face between her hands, Libby let the tears fall. "I love you, too. I have for so long."

"Good. We're agreed then." Evan looked down at her with a grin. "Are you ready to dance with a one-legged cowboy?"

"I'm ready to dance with Superman." She tilted her head and offered him her lips again.

He bent down to meet her and slipped his hands around her

waist while she stretched on tiptoes, wrapping her arms tighter around his neck.

EVAN KISSED Libby's bare shoulder as they danced their third dance. His pulse hiccupped when Libby lifted her face and smiled with heavy-lidded eyes. He'd never seen a more beautiful woman in his life. The scent of her cut through all the cologne and perfume in the room—something sweet and fresh that knocked him off kilter.

Libby tightened her arms around him and hid her nose in his neck. She inhaled and made a noise of approval in her throat that caused a shiver of longing to trip down his spine and land in his belly. "I still can't believe you talked Lefty into moving to the ranch." She slid her arms under his suit jacket, around his waist, and pressed herself tighter to him.

When he was sure he could talk without squeaking, he cleared his throat. "It was Seth's idea. He said Lefty needed to feel like part of the community again and turns out he was right. It works in everybody's favor. Lefty gets a new, custom-build cabin to live in for the rest of his days, a job, and we'll even get him a dog."

"I like that idea." Libby treated him to a brilliant smile that hit him hard behind the knees.

"And you get your home back," he said in a thick voice.

"You didn't have to hire a carpenter to make repairs for me."

"Seth arm-wrestled me for the privilege of paying the guy. I let him win." He kissed the freckles sprinkled across her nose like he'd wanted to do so many times. "Troy does good work. I've hired him to build the retreat compound on a section of the ranch that belongs to me. We poured the foundation for Lefty's cabin there."

"I suppose I'll move to my own house now." Libby hummed as they danced. His hand resting on her back absorbed the low vibration. It felt like she was purring against him.

Evan wished very much that they were alone. Was it hot in here? He took a step back to put some distance between their bodies. "The sight of you stops my heart, darlin'."

Libby gave him a silky look as she pretended to size him up. A tomboy whistle completely at odds with her dress came from her lips and surprised him. "You're looking mighty good, too, Mr. McClure."

The kind of laughter a guy let out when he forgot he was at a swanky party belted out of Evan. It felt good to be in love.

"Attention ladies and cowboys." A voice from the stage stopped the music and the dancers. "Please find your seats. We're going to get the awards ceremony underway."

Evan and Libby held hands on the way back to their table.

Nate sat between Dad and Grandpa Smokey, using silverware and the salt and pepper shakers to illustrate something. He must be telling them war stories. Evan winced and pulled out a chair a few seats down. Libby gave him a grateful smile and sipped the flute of champagne that appeared in front of her by a server who bore an uncanny resemblance to the barista at Jumping Beans Coffee House.

"I'll have a cider," Evan answered the silent question in her eyes.

The server nodded and set a glass of amber liquid in front of Evan.

Lefty, in a neatly pressed suit, sat one table away with Seth, who'd brought Charmaine as his plus one. Charmaine only had about an hour of nice in her. By the end of the evening, she'd be silly drunk and probably leave with another guy. Why did Seth never learn?

Evan turned his attention to the announcer who was calling for the McClure family to come up the steps. It was now or never. He fingered the velvet box in his jacket pocket and turned to Libby. "Will you come up with us?"

Libby's eyes widened. "I can't. I'm not a McClure. You'll be okay, just hold the rail on the way up the steps." She offered him a soft smile meant to reassure.

"Libby, I'm not afraid of falling. Not anymore." He pulled the box from his pocket but kept his hands under the table. "I know I'm doing this all wrong. I should have planned out a more romantic way…but…"

Libby's smile slipped. Her eyes dropped to his shaking hands. "What's wrong?"

Evan gulped air like a trout swallowing a hook and slipped out of his chair to take a knee.

Libby scooted to the edge of her seat. "Evan?" She whispered in an urgent voice.

"Elizabeth Halverson would you do me the honor of becoming my wife? Would you change your last name and make me the happiest man in this room?"

Lips and chin trembling, Libby clasped her hands to her heart and bobbed her head. She choked on a sob and then mustered a watery smile.

"I should have said that I love you first. I've messed this whole thing up." He dropped his head. "This isn't how I planned to do it."

Libby's breath tickled the back of his neck as she placed a light kiss on it. He shuddered and reached for her hand feeling every kind of fool. Legs were moving around them, chairs scraping, as his family headed up to the stage.

Libby's hand came under his jaw, and she lifted his face. "Evan, I don't love you for what you can do or for what you might give me. I love you because of who you are. I admire you, and I can't imagine anyone I'd rather share my life with. Yes, I'd be proud to change my last name and marry you."

Heart prancing, Evan didn't bother to hide how Libby's answer made him feel. He swooped her into his arms and whooped all the way up to the stage with her. He took the stairs two at a time and went straight for the microphone. "She said yes!"

Evan stood with a heart as full as his arms in front of everyone who mattered to him. The crowded room erupted as men jumped to their feet and women clapped.

"You can set me down now," Libby whispered, her face cherry red.

"Oh." Evan set her on her feet. He pulled the twenty-carat radiant-cut diamond ring from its velvet cushion.

Libby's lashes flew wide, her mouth sprung an undiluted smile that made his heart skip. She held out her hand and he slipped the ring on her finger. Her eyes sprung a leak and he pulled her against his chest where she nestled while Dad and his brothers slapped his back.

The announcer stepped in front of the microphone. "It seems the McClures are getting more than a few awards tonight. Everyone congratulate the newly—and I mean very newly—engaged couple."

Epilogue

M
McClure

The McClure-Halverson Wedding

"Is there anything more romantic than a Valentine's Day wedding?" Molly sighed and snuggled Rose closer. Rose, no longer a baby but a toddler with a mind of her own, wanted nothing to do with the stiff dress embroidered with roses and trimmed in faux fur. It matched Bella's dress but Rose didn't care about things like that yet. She'd fussed for the last hour, lost her shoes, and the rosebud wreath pinned in her curls was savaged. Molly worried her lip. Were roses poisonous? She didn't think so. But just in case, she scanned the room for Mom or Grandma Rose. It was entirely possible her toddler might have eaten some of the flowers.

The wedding guests clustered together inside the small

country church. Libby and Evan wanted a country wedding, but country didn't have to mean plain. Josie, always the fashionable one of the three sisters, had come to town like a whirligig. She hadn't even blinked one of her long lashes at spending the Cameron money and ordered hundreds of red roses for the wedding.

Two weeks ago, the bridal shower had featured not only a chocolate fountain but a champagne fountain as well. They'd all worked together to clear Mom's big barn and make it into a rustic venue for the shower. With Josie directing affairs, and Molly in charge of decorations, it had turned into the talk of Apple Valley. Dolly the llama had been a willing photo prop with a feather boa around her neck. Standing in front of a canvas screen for their guests, she was a hit. If you didn't count the incident with the unfortunate Mrs. McGuinty and her former hat.

The Apple Valley Community Church, packed to the rafters, was not dissimilar to a hothouse on Libby and Evan's wedding day. The fresh scent of the flowers collided with the cologne of fifty men so Molly stayed near the door for gulps of fresh air. The old wooden meeting house was the obvious choice for a wedding since Smokey's parents had built it and every McClure had married inside its log walls since.

The jingling of bells from the snow-covered road leading to the church caught Molly's attention and caused a thrill to dance through her. She met Cody's eyes and the warmth in his expression kindled the fire in her heart for her handsome husband. They were going to need to hire a nanny now that they had another baby on the way. But that was her secret, and she'd keep it until after her sister's wedding.

Cody stood up front as Evan's best man, tall and proud in his tux and best boots. Molly smiled in satisfaction when she scanned the front of the room. Every member of the wedding party wore a piece of her jewelry. Grandma Rose had styled her look with a turquoise squash blossom that was sure to be the talk of the entire state once photos of the second McClure-Halverson wedding were released to the papers.

The snorting of a horse, the jangle of bells, and snow-muffled clopping of hooves on the dirt road caused a press of wedding guests to rush the door and windows for a peek at Libby. Molly gave her a reassuring smile from her post at the door.

Libby was a beautiful bride.

She sat tall in the sleigh with her rose-gold hair piled high, woven with pearls and rosebuds. Grandma Rose's vintage cape wrapped her like a gift, hiding her wedding dress, as they'd planned. Libby arranged the cape, allowing it to slip for the photographers to snap peeks at the ivory gown underneath. Alex and Mom had each hired their own photographers and that would be a family joke forever more.

Evan was dashing, and obviously impatient, as he shifted his weight from boot to boot and leaned back, trying to catch a glimpse of his bride. The sleigh was at a full stop in front of the church, in the direct line of vision to the altar. Evan's eyes swam with emotion when he finally caught sight of her. Libby let down one white cowboy boot from the sleigh on her descent to the ground.

Every eye was riveted.

Josie poked Molly in the ribs, startling her. "What did I tell you about those boots?"

Molly nodded without taking her eyes off her other sister. The soles of Libby's boots were painted turquoise, the couple's names and wedding date printed in a curly, white font over it. Pink-hued crystals inlaid in the leather cut-outs of the boot shaft sparkled and glimmered against the snow. Molly grinned as Libby held her foot out longer than necessary, showboating a bit for the photographers.

It was a fairytale day. Libby was finally marrying the man she'd been in love with since they were girls having slumber parties, staying up late to giggle over secret crushes. The guy every girl in town had pined over at one time or another was putting a ring on her sister's finger. Molly sighed again, not caring that she was being dramatic.

Josie sighed too, but when Molly turned to her, Josie's line of vision was directed on another. It wasn't Libby in her stunning gown that Josie was sighing over. Molly couldn't believe Josie was eyeballing *him*. He wasn't her usual type at all.

Molly waved her hand in front of her sister's face and smirked. Josie's eyes shuttered, and she aimed her eyes at Libby, climbing from the sleigh.

The palomino horse pulling the sleigh was a gift from Alex McClure. Libby finally owned her own horse again. Alex came and held the reins steady while Nate McClure stepped forward to assist Libby. Clusters of roses graced the sleigh, tucked into garlands of pine all around the sides. It was simple but stunning. The sharp scent of the greens mingled with the sweet roses. If only they could bottle that, nobody would smell a rose again without remembering Libby and Evan's wedding day.

Libby wore a small, demure smile but Molly wasn't fooled. Her sister was doing cartwheels on the inside.

Nate took Libby's hand, steadying her as she stood near the horse's head on the path the men had shoveled free of snow to the church door. It was a Narnia moment, and thank goodness they had two photographers working together to get shots from different angles.

Nate escorted Libby to Smokey, who held out his arm for her. He walked her inside the church with dignity and a bit of pomp. It was thrilling.

Mom whispered in Bella's ear, then Bella whispered in Theo's. They met solemnly in the center of the aisle and lead the way to the altar. Bella tossed rose petals for Libby to walk over, and Theo carried the ring and led Pumpkin on a leash.

Mom kissed both of Libby's cheeks in a blessing and handed her the bridal bouquet.

Molly wasn't the only one to gasp at the sight of Libby's wedding gown when Mom unclasped the rose brooch at Libby's throat and the cape slid down her shoulders. Mom caught it and handed it to Grandma Rose, who beamed with pleasure just like she'd done at Molly and Cody's wedding. She wore the same silver cowboy boots, too.

Libby turned a smile so wide on her waiting groom that it

was probably cramping her cheeks. Molly happened to see Evan wipe a tear and felt a catch in her throat.

"Libby has never been more beautiful," Josie whispered. She blotted tears, careful of her make-up. She reached for Molly's hand, but Molly sniffed and hid a sneaky swipe to her nose on baby Rose's blanket before she twined her fingers with Josie's. Rose was warm, comforting, and fast asleep on Molly's shoulder.

LIBBY WILTED against Evan's chest. They'd danced all night. Well, she more than he—and her feet were aching. Not that she minded, she'd do it all over again every day if she could. Their wedding day had been the most perfect day of her life. She pressed further into Evan's chest, smiling at the dub-dub, lub-dub of his heart against her ear. She closed her eyes and focused on the rhythm until her heart began to beat in tandem with his. She rested her hands on Evan's shoulders and the thumping of his heart sped up. Molly smiled like a cat in the cream and closed her eyes.

They'd finally gotten away from well-wishers for a moment alone. She'd changed out of her gown before the dancing but she'd kept the gorgeous boots on that Josie had gifted her like they'd been Super Glued to her feet.

Evan shifted her weight and nuzzled her neck. He slid his warm, rough hand over the thin, sensitive skin on the side of her neck and brushed her hair away. His hands on her skin always gave her a delicious shiver. "Don't you think it's time we loaded up the truck and got on the road?" His voice was husky.

"Eager to begin the honeymoon, are you?" She teased with a husky tone of her own.

"I certainly am eager, Mrs. McClure."

"Oh, Evan. I love that. Say it again." Libby swiveled her body around and placed her hands on his collarbones. Their eyes locked. Delightful shocks coursed through her at the desire in his gaze. "I love you so much," she whispered before she touched her mouth to Evan's. She twined her hands around the back of his neck to pull him closer.

Evan kissed her back, pressed her to his chest until her lungs flattened. Who needed air? She was wrapped in the arms of her Superman and wanted nothing else. Well, except maybe a little Evan Jr. by this time next year.

The End

Afterword

My Scottish-Irish family came west in 1890. They homesteaded in Colorado, where I was eventually born. My great-grandmother was born in the tent in this photo. I come from a long line of tough ranchers and railroad men. It's fun to write stories set in small towns with tight communities. My hope is you will enjoy your visit and become part of the community.

One of my favorite family members to hear about was Belle. My great-aunt was a lady rancher who worked hard and even rode broncs. She was once featured in her local newspaper for "brawling in the street."

Gram, or Rowdy Rosey, reminds me of Belle. The funny thing is, I wrote Gram years ago, before I ever "met" Belle.

I love the Western culture and I'm proud to come from strong people. It's my joy to introduce you to characters who have grit, grace, and lots of foibles. I hope you see something to admire or relate to.

God bless and keep you,

Dalyn

P.S. Reviews and ratings help books stand out in an ocean of books. If you are kind enough to take the time to recommend my books, ask your local librarian to order them, or rate/review on Amazon, Goodreads, Bookbub, or anywhere else, I'd be appreciative. I'd also love to hear about it. Please drop me a line or tag me in a post because I'd love the chance to thank you.

Acknowledgments

I'd like to thank my editor and friend, Pegg Thomas for encouraging me to rise up to my best work. You're an inspiration to me and I love your stories.

Susie May Warren, you're a great teacher. Thanks for giving so much of yourself and being so genuine.

Elizabeth Bråten, thank you for being willing brainstorm even though we live on different continents. Thank goodness for technology! I'm grateful to call you a friend. Keep writing your stories of lands exotic to me and I'll keep writing those that seem exotic to you!

Thank you, Jocelyn LaMay for catching all the little foxes.

A special thank you to my husband, Doug, for giving me time, space, and resources to write these books. And for providing excellent material for the kissing scenes. *wink wink*

About the Author

I live on a small horse ranch with my very own tall, dark, & handsome, on a dirt road in central Washington's high desert region of the Pacific Northwest. We have a few kids and grandkids and too many houseplants.

I'm a bit of a foodie, a terrible coffee snob, and a book addict.

I believe inspirational romance stories are a shadow of The Great Romance. Jesus is the ultimate hero!

I love to hear from readers. Please sign up for my newsletter, where I share news first,

have exclusive sneak peaks and have giveaways.
Visit me on social media, and let's be friends.

Dalyn Weller

facebook.com/DalynWellerAuthor

twitter.com/dalynweller

instagram.com/dalynweller

pinterest.com/dalynweller

goodreads.com/DalynWeller

bookbub.com/authors/dalyn-weller

amazon.com/author/dalynweller

Also by Dalyn Weller

The Rancher's Surprise Second Chance

Fashioned For Love

Love Happens At Sweetheart Farm

LOVE HAPPENS AT

Sweetheart
♥ *Farm* ♥

Dalyn Weller

A PACIFIC NORTHWEST ROMANCE